JUST ANOTHER
SLEEPING
BEAUTY

SUSAN KOHLER

CCB Publishing
British Columbia, Canada

Just Another Sleeping Beauty

Copyright ©2018 by Susan Kohler
ISBN-13   978-1-77143-364-8
First Edition

Library and Archives Canada Cataloguing in Publication
Kohler, Susan, 1950-, author
Just another sleeping beauty / by Susan Kohler. -- First edition.
Issues in print and electronic formats.
ISBN 978-1-77143-364-8 (pbk.).--ISBN 978-1-77143-365-5 (pdf)
Additional cataloguing data available from Library and Archives Canada

Publisher: CCB Publishing
British Columbia, Canada
www.ccbpublishing.com

This is dedicated to two people who saved me, in many ways.

I have not had a family for nearly 30 years,
until they made me part of theirs,
with patience and love.

Thank you, Dawn and Michael.

Prologue

Love endures, a soul will find its mate, over centuries, throughout the world, because love endures. There are always obstacles that make finding that love, that mate for the soul, even sweeter. Sometimes the obstacles are rooted in evil. An evil that must be fought and defeated for love to grow. It may be that a soul mate is not found in one life, but is hidden in another time or another place. Love will always win over evil, maybe not in the here and now, but eventually love will win, with God's help.

Don't believe me? Just ask Robbie McDougal. Whenever he is.

Chapter One

Robbie

Robbie McDougal stood quietly, pausing as he looked out over the Loch, admiring the green hills, rugged cliffs and the dark, deep blue of the water. He was a handsome man, with long black hair and blazing blue eyes. His features were chiseled but not rough, and his build was trim but still muscular. He wore his breacan-an-feileadh with style. He seemed to always have a lass around him.

And why not? He was a champion at the Highland games, held to select men to guard the laird, and protect the clan. He was not undefeated but was known for winning with a surprising regularity. He had the perfect balance of strength needed for the heavy events such as the caber toss where a log is held upright in a man's hands while he runs forward and tosses it, the stone put, or the hammer throw. He also had the combination of the patience and endurance for the Maide-leisg, an event that calls for the two men to be sitting on the ground with the soles of their feet pressing each other, with each holding the end of a stick between their hands which they pulled against each other until one of them was raised from the ground. He was also fleet of foot and often won the footraces run up a steep slope.

He had no talent for the bagpipes, although he loved the sound of them, especially when he followed them into battle. In peace, he preferred listening to the fiddle and drums. He could sing with a fine tenor, usually after a few drinks in the local pub. He loved watching the dancers, especially when they were competing, rather than joining in with them. He watched the maidens particularly closely. He was fine in a fight, with fist or sword, winning very often and more or less gracious in defeat.

He was a great horseman, with a firm, steady seat on a horse at any speed. He trained his horses to be very responsive to his slightest commands. He loved making daring raids on other clans, usually stealing horses, which were often later stolen back. When the other clan did steal the horses back, they were better trained, in better condition, and the mares were usually with foal by his stallion.

He often dispensed justice for his father. He could be calm and steady when needed and was a fair judge when called on, but he was ruthless when it was called for. He had been raised to rule, with consideration when needed, and action when required, but was by nature more prone to decisive action.

* * *

That morning he had crawled out of a bed he had shared with Gynne, a sweet lass always eager to join him in bed. As he kissed pretty Gynne goodbye, giving her plump bottom a friendly farewell pinch, he had no idea that he was watched by a jealous friend, more than just a friend, his cousin, Dauid.

He thought of Dauid as his best friend and trusted him. They had bonded over many a fight, drunken brawl or raiding party. Some of the fights were against a common enemy and some against each other. Both men had bloodied the other, and blackened his eye, before hugging and each drinking another tankard of ale. In truth, they had shared many nights in the pub drinking.

One night they had such a great brawl in the pub, that others joined in and several tables were smashed to kindling. The brawl stopped when ale began to be spilled. No point wasting good ale, was there?

There was one thing that bothered Robbie's father, the McDougal. He did not trust Dauid. In fact, he warned Robbie to be wary of his friend.

"I admire your loyalty to your cousin Dauid," he said. "But I sense some jealousy in him. I think he will betray ye some fine day."

"I do not wish to defy ye, father, but I feel ye are wrong," Robbie answered, still respectful, even when disagreeing with his father.

Robbie and Dauid had kissed and bedded many of the same maidens. One fine night, Robbie bedded the usually cheerful Gynne, while Dauid had his way with red-headed Mariore, before switching partners. Unfortunately, Gynne was in no mood to be switched off to Dauid, and she gave him an earful and a sharp slap.

The third member of their little group was Thome. He loved Robbie as if they were brothers, and like the laird had sought to warn Robbie about Dauid. Soon after Thome spoke his fears to Robbie, he disappeared and could not be found. Robbie certainly had no idea of the danger he was in or the depths of evil to which his jealous cousin could sink.

* * *

He continued his hike, around the loch and up the craggy green hills to the witch's cottage. Rosie the witch was not a crone or evil, as many thought of a witch. She was old, around her fiftieth year, but her eyes were merry, her step lively, and her love for her daughter without bounds. She did no evil spells, but was kind, healing and helping those who came to her. She delivered babes and comforted the dying. The people of her clan loved and trusted her.

As Robbie approached her hut, she came out to greet him. On this day her blue eyes were clouded with concern and pain.

"Rosie, what's wrong?" he asked filled with concern for her, unused to seeing her so worried.

"'Tis nothing, my boy," she replied, forcing a smile. "I am just having a bit of an off day. Come in, Robbie, and have a glass of ale with me."

"I will nae turn that down." Robbie smiled as he entered her small hut.

Robbie sat at her small table. Rosie had two tankards of ale already poured and put one in front of him reluctantly, with a great sadness in her soft blue eyes. Vaguely he wondered why she already had his ale poured. How had she known he was coming?

"I am sorry, Robbie," she said as he began to drink, "truly sorry."

Soon, Robbie's head began to swim. "What? Did ye do something to me? I thought ye were my friend."

"I am, Robbie," she said before he started losing consciousness. "I am but I had no choice. Dauid kidnapped my daughter and told me that to get her back, I had to kill ye, else she would die."

"So I am dying then?" He fought to hold on to consciousness.

"No, Robbie, I could not do that, I love ye too much." She had tears in her eyes. "Ye will look dead, seem to be dead, and your body will be buried but ye will not die. Ye will remain in dreams, and ye can emerge from those dreams into real life again."

"How?" he managed, he was fading fast.

"Ye will need to find love, real love, in the dreams."

Robbie seemed to die, not knowing what happened next. Thome found him seemingly dead, and dug a grave to bury him. Rosie caught Thome before he had a chance to bury Robbie, and told him not to bury him because he was not really dead. They found a body so mangled as to be unrecognizable and substituted it for Robbie's. His parents were devastated. The whole of the clan mourned. The witch Rosie was blamed and accused of poisoning him. At first, she was too proud to run and hide, but

Thome took her to safety. Once there, she buried Robbie in a shallow unmarked grave.

Thome knew well she loved Robbie as if he were her son. He told the king that she had killed herself to avoid capture and he had buried her. Thome found her daughter for her. They agreed the girl would be safer if she were kept away from Rosie. He arranged for the girl to be taken in and raised by a good, kind family. So Rosie was hidden away but alive and unhurt, and took comfort in knowing her daughter was safe.

The laird told Dauid, who had not been seen in the village since Robbie's apparent death, that Rosie had killed herself in grief for the killing of Robbie. Almost against his better judgment, he named Dauid as his heir to become the laird of the clan. Although the McDougal was in deep mourning, he began to teach Dauid to be his heir, but he still yearned for his son out of fatherly love and also because of his recognition of his son's abilities. Not just in strength and fighting, nor just in bedding women, but for his judgment and good sense. He always had a maturity that put the good of the clan ahead of himself, and the McDougal knew that Dauid would not do so, that he would always care for himself first.

* * *

Robbie seemed to float in his coffin. He felt no pain or fear, no heat or cold, and no need for food, air or water. He had no sense of self or of the passage of time. From time to time he became aware of another presence and he would communicate with them in thoughts, getting to know them and then, soon, inevitably they would be gone. They would fade from his memory and he would be alone once again. Most of the women were easily forgotten.

Then after several women had come and gone, he began to sense someone else, another woman. She was once again, not really with him, but a presence. She was a young woman, very attractive, slender with brown hair and green eyes. She lay on a bed, in a small cottage. She seemed ill, confused, and very sad.

Still, she seemed to be very pleasant company, a bit sad but friendly, and before long he remembered that he was meant to find true love here in the land of dreams in order to truly live again. Was she the one? He hoped she was.

He could picture her in his mind as she was before her illness. One of the things he noted was her rare way of dressing, which seemed very strange to him. It was not the same dresses he was used to seeing on the women of his clan. Her clothes were not the rich gowns of a noble lady but seemed well made and of decent fabric. The clothes were not ornate but looked well on her.

He spoke to her in his thoughts. Her replies came to him in his own language, but he knew they were coming from her in a foreign tongue. Her speech had a musical accent, completely different from anything he had ever heard and he enjoyed it. He began to ask her questions about her life, but she stopped him.

"Before I say anything to you about my life, I want to hear more about yours." She thought, but not unkindly. "These are treacherous times and I do not choose to give any information to a stranger, even in my dreams."

"I am Robbie McDougal of the clan McDougal," he answered patiently. "I was sent here, into what I call the land of shadows and dreams, in the year of our Lord 1584. I come from the Highlands."

"Why?" she asked.

"Why what?" He smiled his answer.

"Why were you sent here, and how?" she asked again.

"I was sent here by a witch. She was seeking to protect me from a coward and a traitor," he explained. "I was told that were I to find true love I would go back to the land of the living. Now, will ye tell me about yourself?"

6

"I am Marie, a dressmaker to the Queen." She paused and continued sadly, "The former queen."

"How did ye come to be here? I mean, in this place with no form, no time, and barely any life?" he asked.

"I fell ill, I know not why, but I lost all sense of self," Marie explained.

"Where are we? And in what year?" he asked.

"This is Paris, France in the year 1794."

"I have been in a grave for one hundred and ten years?" Robbie was shocked.

"You have come to me at a very bad time. We are in the midst of a revolution." She seemed sad. "To overthrow the government. The king and queen have been executed, and now it seems as if there is no law and anyone can be taken and killed for no reason. Many have gained a sick desire for blood and human suffering."

"There is no law to protect ye?" He was shocked.

"Only what is called a reign of terror."

"Why did this start?" He was puzzled.

"There are many reasons," she told him. "I think one of the major reasons is that the peasants are angry. They feel the king and queen live in luxury, and do nothing but spend money, money the peasants have worked hard to gain. Meanwhile, many of them have no money for food or shelter for their families. Their children are starving."

"Do they not believe that rulers should have wealth?" he asked.

"Well, some think everyone should have the same things. But..." She paused, searching for words.

"But-" he prompted.

"But I do not. I think rulers should work hard for their people and if they do they deserve some of the symbols of their rank, but I also believe all people who work hard, at any task, deserve to have the advantage of their hard work."

"That sounds fair, did the king and queen not agree?"

"The king and queen were thoughtless about their subjects. They saw us as tools, hardly human. All they seemed to care about was living a lavish life with luxuries such as grand houses and jewels, not about us."

"Yet ye worked for the queen." He asked, "What was she like?"

"I needed the job, and I am a good seamstress. The queen was not unpleasant to me, but she was vain and careless with people and things." She paused. "She really loved her children. I do not believe she should have been executed."

He asked, "What would ye have wanted to happen to her?"

"I believe she should have been stripped of her crown, her money and her privilege. Few ever saw her without fancy gowns and powdered wigs, so she would not be recognized. She could have been put in a small cottage, such as many live in, and made to fend for herself."

Robbie never knew how long they talked, but she seemed to slowly overcome her illness and began to gain strength; it gave him hope. She was a good companion, warm, gentle and caring. Still, there was a sadness to her he could not understand. Nevertheless, she showed him glimpses of the city, Paris, as it had been before the Revolution. He saw the grandeur of the palace grounds, and many statues and fountains. He saw pubs and restaurants. And he saw crushing poverty. Then she showed him how it looked now, and he saw destruction everywhere, oceans of blood in the streets, and fear and hatred among the people. He felt their fierce anger but could find no direction for it.

One day, after she regained her health, he was surprised to see she was crying.

"What is wrong Marie?" he asked.

"I have been charged with treason," she said softly.

"They cannae convict ye, ye hae done nothing wrong," he tried to reassure her.

"There will be no trial." She stopped weeping, her eyes red and swollen as she told him, "Being charged is the same as being convicted."

It was then that he realized her body was no longer in the cottage but in a cell, a dirty, dank cell with a foul-smelling, straw-covered floor, and infested with vermin.

"How long will ye remain imprisoned in this place?" he asked.

Her answer was sad, as she told him, "For the rest of my life. Not long, not nearly long enough."

Her reply filled him with dread and anger. Still, he did his best to comfort her and soon realized that he had fallen in love with her. He fought the knowledge of her impending death. There had to be a way to escape her fate. Surely, she was the one he was supposed to love.

He was aware that every day the guards came and took people out of the prison cells. Some went quietly, some cried, and some fought every step of the way, screaming, but all were terrified. He began to fear for her even as he admired her courage and spirit. He felt some love for her and gave her what comfort he could. He stayed with her as long as he could but one day the guards came and she was taken out of her cell. She went with courage, dignity, and resignation. His spirit followed and watched as she was taken to a strange structure. Then he saw it, as she was executed on the guillotine.

He felt her soft kiss, before she faded and crossed over. He was grief-stricken, screaming in rage and pain. He lost all hope, and his soul returned to the grave.

* * *

He stayed alone, in his own private hell. Since he had no sense of time, he did not know how long he was alone. Eventually, he found another young woman with him. Once again, she seemed very ill. As soon as he noticed her, he forgot his grief and shock over Marie's death, although he never forgot Marie.

He looked around before speaking to this young woman and noticed she was in was a crude, hostile environment, very dirty and dusty. She was lying on some blankets on the ground, near a campfire. There were several strange looking wagons in a circle surrounding her.

She wore crude, almost worn through clothes, and a bonnet was on the ground beside her. She had dirty, stringy blond hair and brown eyes. He could not tell where they were, but he could feel a tough air about her, with courage, determination, and defiance mixed.

When she became aware of his presence, her first question for him was, "Who are you and why are you here?"

He could not place her accent as he replied simply, "I am Robbie McDougal of the clan McDougal, and I do not know, really, why I am here but I do know ye are very ill, on the verge of death. My questions are: who are ye? Also, where is this place and what year is it?"

She told him, "I am Kate, the year is 1846, and we are in America, in a state called Utah."

"I have never heard of America." He asked simply, "Where is it?"

"It is probably easier if I can tell you how to get here from wherever you came from. Where are you from?" she asked.

"I am from Scotland, the Highlands," he said proudly.

"Well, America is very far away from Scotland, across the Atlantic Ocean, to the west."

"And, Lass, why are you here in this barren country?" He was curious.

"I am traveling in a wagon train across America to a place called California to start a new life."

He was puzzled, usually the women he spoke to were single,

but surely a single woman would not be on such a journey traveling by herself. "Are you alone on your journey? No husband? No family?"

"Yes, I am alone now, but I hope to meet up with some people in California."

"How did ye become ill?" he asked gently.

"Our wagon train was attacked by Indians, and I was injured. The wound has badly festered and made me ill."

"So ye are near India?" This was puzzling to him.

"No," She laughed softly. "The Indians in America are not really Indians. Someone who thought this was India began to call them that, and the name stuck. They are natives of this land," she explained.

She took his hand and showed him some of the east coast. He saw some large cities and fertile farmland, some truly beautiful countryside.

"Most of the people you see were born here but this country started as an English colony," she explained. "Almost fifty years ago there was a war with England. We wanted Independence, so we fought for it, well, the founding fathers fought for it. We kicked the king out and formed our own country. We do not have a king, we are a republic."

"Who are those dark-skinned people? I hae never seen anyone like them," he asked with curiosity.

"They are Negros. Most of them are slaves. Many were born here but their ancestors came from Africa, a continent south of Europe. Some were kidnapped and sold into slavery, then brought here. Most black men and women in the south are slaves. Some in other parts of the country are free."

"Ye hae slaves in this country?" He was shocked.

"I hate slavery, but yes, we do have slaves in the southern states. Many people want to end slavery but the people who own slaves refuse to give them up. They see the slaves as, well, as farm animals. It's so wrong, they are like other men and deserve the same rights as anyone else. I fear the debate over slavery will lead to a war." She sounded sad.

"To end slavery?"

"Not only for that reason, there are many different things states disagree on, one of them is slavery," she said. "As I said, I detest slavery but I want to end it without a war. I fear that will not happen and many lives will be lost in the battle."

Then she showed him, as well as she could what the west coast was like, before admitting, "Of course I have not been there yet, so I may have some things wrong."

Next, she showed him around the wagon train and gave him some facts. "We left a place called Springfield, Illinois in mid-April. We made stops along the way and joined a large wagon train captained by William Russell about 100 miles west of a town called Independence. Our wagon train is called the Donner party. Now, at its largest, I think we have over 80 people."

"Why such a large group?" he wondered.

"For protection against the natives," she said quietly.

"Ye mean the Indians?" He laughed.

"Yes, the natives attack wagons traveling alone, they are fierce warriors. They hate and mistrust the white men, and with good reason. That's why we circle the wagons at night, for protection."

"So this is a dangerous journey?"

"Yes, it is, very dangerous and arduous. We have lost some people along the way. Still, we have people traveling with their families and everything they own, including dogs, horses, and oxen, even chickens and goats. All the furniture we hope to bring is packed in the wagons, and some has had to be discarded along the way."

As they looked around he saw the cook fires near each wagon. He saw the families together around their wagons and other groups. The next day he saw some of the men go hunting for the large creatures they called buffaloes. He also saw them hunt deer, bears, and rabbits.

After the men came back from hunting, they loaded her back into the wagon and left the camp. Later that day, they crossed a river almost losing a wagon, and he realized how truly dangerous it was. Still, the people in the train forged ahead.

A few days later they had to climb a steep hill with some very rough terrain, causing a wagon to break an axle, and a horse to break its leg. He saw them shoot the horse and butcher it. They also tossed out the fine looking furniture from the wagon with the broken axle.

Although he felt an admiration for the woman and liked her, he did not love her. Still, he was disappointed when she died in her sleep.

* * *

The next time he was conscious of a woman's presence it really amazed him. He was told the time period was called the Roaring Twenties, the 1920s, and the place was called Chicago. He did not get to look around this time. He heard people talking about something called prohibition, which seemed to be a ban on drinking. That amazed him, how could they ban whiskey and ale? There were thoughts about places called speakeasies, where people broke that ban. Women called flappers danced something called the Charleston. He looked and saw the really strange dress, short and wildly ornate, covered with strings that moved about as the women danced. It was very bizarre to him, the music seemed strident and overly cheerful as if someone was trying to convince the listener that everything was wonderful when it was not.

The woman he met there was in a coma after an injury. She had been shot by gangsters. When he tried to connect with her, she was hostile and distant, and very angry at almost everyone. Moreover, he could sense her death. He was sympathetic to her but she rejected the very idea of another being in her coma with her, so he left. It was the only time he failed to even have a nice chat with one of the women he found in his dreams, and he felt even more alone and defeated than he ever had.

Chapter Two

Cynthia

Cynthia Snowden sat on the balcony off her bedroom sipping the tea her housekeeper, Rosie, had brought her. Rosie was a source of care and comfort to Cyn. She'd come in and patted Cyn on the shoulder before giving her the tea. Cyn looked up into Rosie's soft blue eyes and smiled sadly. She had come to depend on Rosie, a plump, motherly woman in her early sixties, with a warm smile and quiet, loving manner. She had become much more than a housekeeper to Cyn, especially in the recent months, since her life had become so crazy and confusing.

From the second floor, Cyn could look out over the rose garden and listen to the fountain below and relax. The small balcony gave her some peace from her chaotic life. It was rare for her to have any solitude, any peace, but it was sometimes very necessary.

Things had changed in her life in the few months since the sudden and unexpected death of her father. She'd had to suppress her grief and mourning to handle everything that came to her with his passing. She was still very young, just a few months shy of twenty-one, and now very rich. She had inherited her father's fortune of several million dollars. She also had his sprawling horse ranch, with both racing thoroughbreds and pleasure horses, and his condo in town. She would gladly give it all up just to see her father again for a minute. Of course, she had also inherited his problems and responsibilities. The problems included her stepmother and two stepsisters, along with seven half- and stepbrothers. The responsibilities were overseeing his businesses, the ranch, and caring for the boys.

Her father had been a prudent man. Although he was in excellent health, he had thought long and hard to plan for any eventuality. He spoke to his attorney and his advisers to decide what should be set in place, just in case. He had started divorce proceedings against his fourth wife, Gertrude, but she had him mired in a morass of court procedures and delays. Secretly he thought, no feared, Gertrude would rather be his widow than his ex-wife.

His first wife, Cynthia's mother, had died of cancer when she was a little girl, only four. The loss devastated him. His second wife had also died young, in a car crash, leaving him with three young stepsons. He loved the boys. His third wife proved extremely fertile and fickle. She'd given him two boys, then a set of twins. One day she ran off with another man leaving him with the boys.

That's why he tried to plan for anything because he knew full well how life could hit you with the unexpected. He had personal security and a private investigator watching out against that eventuality. He had tried to set everything up for his family. He had hired a motherly housekeeper, Rosie, and two young people to run the household, provide child care for the boys, and companionship for Cynthia. Johnny was an expert with horses, he oversaw the stables, both the riding horses and the breeding stock. He loved horses and ran the stables with a knowledge that seemed out of place with his young age. Jamie was a competitive swimmer and a certified lifeguard, who was studying early childhood development in her college courses. Johnny and Jaime were twins, with blond hair and blue eyes, in their early twenties.

The three hired staff took care of the boys, but Cynthia was involved in every aspect of their lives, not from duty, but from love. Cynthia's stepmother, Gertrude, acted like she was the lady of the manor, in spite of the fact she had only inherited ten dollars from the will. Her stepsisters, Bridget and Bianca, each got one hundred thousand dollars in a trust. The boys had both college savings and trust funds. Cynthia was set up with a financial adviser but no trust fund to control her spending, a sign of her father's complete trust in her level-headed common sense, maturity, and her ingrained sense of responsibility.

Cynthia lived at the ranch, although she was due to drive into the city that evening for some meetings and dinner with friends. She had called ahead to have the condo made ready for her. It would be good to get away for a day.

She thought about her day. It was typical of her days lately. She had early morning phone meetings with several people from her late father's businesses. As soon as the boys realized she was awake, they began demanding to go riding. She called down to the stables and had Johnny saddle and warm up the horses. Cynthia worked on schooling her horse, Boston, on rail work, and over trail obstacles. Most of the boys wanted to run timed gymkhana courses, wanting the speed and competition of barrel racing and pole bending. Two of the boys, Will and Danny, were more interested in riding English and schooling their horses over low jumps. At the end of the ride, all the boys unsaddled their horses and put up their saddles. They fastened their horses to the hot walker so the horses could cool off safely.

Next, all seven boys wanted to go for a swim. She called Jamie to meet her at the pool, to help supervise the boys in the water. She knew how hectic and wild the seven boys could be in the pool. It was an hour filled with splashing and laughter. Fred and Billy got into a minor spat, so they were told to get out of the pool. When the rest of the boys were done swimming, Cyn told the boys to get dressed and ready for lunch.

Everyone sat down to eat lunch. Gertrude, Bridget, and Bianca joined them. Of course, for the three women, it was really breakfast since they all slept until noon. Gertrude seemed to think she had some control over how the household was run. She spent the whole meal complaining about this and that and giving orders to Cynthia, the boys, Johnny and Jamie, and the housekeeper Rosie. She even bossed around her two daughters.

The breaking point, for Cynthia, was hearing Gertrude say, "I have several brochures for you to look over Cindy, dear. There are some excellent boarding schools for the boys and some colleges for you to transfer to."

"Why would I transfer colleges, Gertrude?" she asked with her teeth clenched.

"So you can attend a top-rated school, maybe UCLA or USC, and have a real college experience in a dorm with parties and friends." She smiled falsely at Cynthia as she mentioned two colleges far away from the ranch in Tennessee. "You have too many responsibilities for your age. You should be having fun."

"And why would I send my brothers off to a boarding school?" she asked, masking her anger.

"Well, dear, you are too young for such a huge responsibility, and I am simply too busy to take care of the boys. Even Bianca and Bridget are too busy." She was filled with phony concern.

"Yes, they are so busy they sleep until noon before shopping and going to a club." Cynthia dropped all pretense. "Understand this, Gertrude: you have no say in where I attend college or where the boys live. None. They will stay with me and I will gladly care for them. They are not a burden, I love them, but you are a burden. I am going to speak with my attorney to have you evicted, even more, to have you erased from my life. Father hated you before he died."

"My attorney tells me I could take everything from you due to your youth," Gertrude shot back.

"Try it, bitch." Cynthia got up from the table and walked slowly and apparently calmly out of the room. The boys followed her. Some of them crying over the scene at lunch.

"Are you going to send us away, Cyn?" Timmy, one of the younger boys asked, his voice wavering.

"No love," she said it softly, hugging his small frame. "I love you all."

As Cynthia reflected on that lunch she realized she hated Gertrude, had hated her, even before her father's death. Now that she suspected Gertrude was behind his sudden death, hate seemed too mild a word for it. She got along fairly well with Bridget and Bianca, they seemed not to be evil and greedy, but they also weren't very smart and certainly had no ambitions. It was summer now, but Cynthia would be going back to college in the fall taking courses in business administration and animal husbandry.

The stables were not just for riding horses for the family. They had a few thoroughbred broodmares and a very well-bred champion stallion. There were pastures for the broodmares and their frisky foals. They also had accommodations for the mares who came in for breeding with their stallion. Johnny was in charge of all the horses, in spite of his duties with the boys. He ran his crew with an iron hand but he was very gentle with the horses.

The pool area was fenced and locked, so either Jamie or Cynthia or both had to be present to let the boys swim. There was also a tennis court and a tennis pro who came out twice a week to give the boys lessons. Cynthia laughed to herself because even with all they had: the horses, the pool and the tennis courts, the boys still kept them busy with other things. Billy and Jimmy played soccer, Timmy loved to play baseball, Fred was into basketball with a good chance to make the team when he got to high school, Will wanted to play football, Henry loved to golf, and Danny was into karate. Cynthia had joined her brother in karate. Cynthia, Rosie, and the twins were kept busy driving them to meets, games, lessons, and appointments. Not only had Gertrude refused to drive the boys anywhere, she had never come to one of their games. Bridget and Bianca had also stayed away. Secretly, Cyn was glad they left the boys alone.

Sighing, Cynthia got up and went inside to get ready for her evening in the city. She planned to have some friends over to the condo for the evening. Before they came she had a meeting with the private investigator. He had worked for her father, and she'd hired him to investigate her father's death. In the morning she had planned a meeting with her attorney. Gertrude was trying to break the will. She was claiming Cynthia was too young for the responsibility of managing her father's businesses, as well as caring for his estate and the boys. She also said Cynthia was on drugs and a party girl. In fact, she even tried to accuse Cynthia of exerting undue pressure on her ailing father, forcing him into making his will carelessly, cutting Gertrude out almost completely, and leaving Cynthia a fortune without even bothering to set her up with a tightly controlled trust fund, and naming Gertrude as the trustee.

Cynthia called the woman who cooked and kept the house tidy when she stayed at the condo and had her fix dinner for four, with some finger food and cold drinks ready before they arrived. As Cyn left the ranch Rosie walked her to the door.

"Please be careful in town, Cyn, I have a terrible feeling that you are in danger." She seemed unsettled, her eyes filled with concern.

"I have been in danger since my father died," Cyn said quietly, "and I think you know why."

"I am afraid that I will never see you again." Rosie's eyes filled with unshed tears as she watched Cyn drive away.

Cyn was ready when the P.I. arrived. She offered him a bite or two to eat from a tray full of cheese and crackers, vegetables with hummus, and fruit. She had put some wine out for him and a cold cola for herself. He poured himself a glass of wine, fixed a small plate of cheese, and poured her the cola. Then he got down to his report.

"As you know, Cyn, because Gertrude was still legally his wife when she ordered his body cremated, they followed her orders," he began, his brown eyes filled with concern. "There was an autopsy, and the coroner was suspicious enough to put the cause of death down as: undetermined. Gertrude doesn't know it but he kept tissue and blood samples to send out for more testing. Those results are not in yet."

"She killed him, I know it." Cyn's fury was barely held in check. "Those lab results will prove it, you'll see."

"I'm sure they will prove murder, but not who murdered him." Anger tightened his face.

"You don't think I..." Cyn began.

"Of course not, but she will try it. Be prepared for it. She will use it to try to take your brothers' and your inheritance away," he warned her.

"She will fail." Cyn was unshakable.

"Yes, I believe she will." He paused with a tight grin on his face, highlighting his chocolate skin. "I've looked into her history. She was married three times before, in different states, and with some changes in her appearance. So far no one has connected it together but she is a widow three times over and each time the death was unexpected, and each time she came away with a large inheritance. Your father was by far the richest man she ever married but she miscalculated with him. He loved you and his sons, and soon came to hate her." He paused. "Don't worry, your lawyer and I will make sure we find enough evidence to have her arrested and tried. The police and coroner's office are suspicious too. She will not get away with it this time. My only worry is that until she is arrested, you have to act naturally around her and not let her see your hatred and suspicions."

"Don't you worry, Lewis, I can hide my suspicions quite well, and if I stop showing my hatred, she'll definitely know something's wrong." Cyn stood and walked the P.I. to the door.

Soon after that David, her current boyfriend, came over. He was movie star handsome, with blond hair and green eyes, a body lean with muscles, and a great smile. He was also well spoken, caring and considerate. They met when he brought a mare to the ranch to be bred, shortly before her father died, and soon started dating. He was wealthy, but not near her father's level. Cyn thought he was a good date, but not perfect. His only fault was that he was pushing Cyn too hard to have sex with him. Cyn did not believe in sex before marriage, even in the twenty-first century. She had faith and values.

After her father died David was supportive and considerate, to a certain point. Cyn noticed that he also seemed to become more demanding, almost controlling. He still wanted sex, but now he was pushing her for a quick marriage, at a time when she had no time or patience to even think about getting married.

When he arrived that night, he hugged Cyn and kissed her hello before sitting beside her on the leather sofa.

"Sweetheart," he said, putting an arm around her shoulders, "let's elope soon so that I can help you in this difficult time."

"Help me?" She turned to look at him. "How can you help me?"

"I can help you with the estate, maybe selling the ranch, and taking care of the boys." He smiled at her and leaned over to kiss her. "I have business experience too, so I can be of help there."

"My businesses are under control," she said softly but with some heat hidden in the words. "The boys are well cared for, and I am keeping the ranch. If I marry, it will be for love, not for someone to manage my life."

"You're being difficult, Ger..." He shut up instantly but it was enough, it set off alarm bells in Cynthia, although she pretended not to notice.

Did David know Gertrude? Had he discussed Cyn with her? Cyn knew she had to find out. His desire to help her manage her inheritance had already aroused her suspicions. She had been warned by her father and his advisers. They spoke about men who would try just that. Men who would run through her money and then leave her with debts. Of course, it would take a great deal of time before he could run through all her money. She had even been warned that a fortune hunter could decide to make her

22

disappear permanently. She was young but not naïve.

Cyn kept her thoughts to herself as the doorbell rang. It was her friends, Amy and Tom. They came in and exchanged hugs before sitting down in her living room and munching on the appetizers.

Cyn had only known Tom, Amy's fiancé, for about a year. He had visited the ranch and she saw him at the college, but he had never been to the condo before so she showed him around quickly. She was proud of it, the way she had blended looks and comfort with durability to stand up to the seven boys.

Tom was tall and lanky, quiet with a shy smile and a sly sense of humor. Cyn liked him. Amy was a childhood friend, a petite brown-eyed blond with a great sense of humor and a quick wit. She knew Cyn inside-out and loved her. Cyn tried to put on a friendly face for her guests but Amy could tell her friend was upset. When they finished eating, she helped Cyn carry dishes out to the kitchen. They talked quietly while they rinsed the dishes and loaded the dishwasher.

"What's wrong Cyn?" she asked quietly. "I can tell something's bothering you, and it's more than the stress you've been under since... well, since."

Cyn closed the dishwasher and started it. "You always know, don't you?"

They sat at the kitchen table. Cyn continued, "It's David. He's always pushing me to have sex with him, and you know how I feel about sex before marriage, but now he's stopped pushing for that and is trying to persuade me to marry him."

"And that is making you unhappy?" Amy questioned, puzzled.

"Well he mentioned, almost insisted, helping me manage my inheritance. It sounded very patronizing, you know, like, 'Don't worry your pretty head about the businesses little lady, I can take care of things,' you know what I mean?"

"Not good." Amy grinned. "How long will he be limping?"

"Right now, he's not limping." She grinned back. "But he's not going to get what he wants either. To top it off, he started to mention Gertrude, but realized his mistake, shut up and backed off."

"Really, not good," Amy said with no trace of humor.

"Amy, check the door won't you?" Cyn pulled out her phone. "I want to make a quick call."

"That David doesn't know about?" Amy looked grim, before continuing, "The guys have a baseball game on. Men! They're not paying any attention to us."

"Keep watch for me."

Cyn dialed the P.I. and made a quick request, "Lewis, please do a background check on David Fulsom. I need information on his financial status, including how he got it. I also need to find out if he has any ties to Gertrude. Please, and do it as soon as you can. Thanks a lot."

"Let's take dessert out to the guys," Cyn said. "I have lemon cake."

Later, she had a bit of a struggle but she did manage to push David out when her friends left, with a promise to think about his offer of help.

"Let me stay and we can talk about getting married," David said, sitting very close to Cyn.

"No, David, please go home. I'm very tired right now. Please let me think without pressure. Then I can be sure of my feelings and happy with my answer when I give it to you. Please, honey." She used the endearment with distaste.

David pushed a bit more, trying seduction and even a little force to convince her to let him stay.

"David," she said sweetly as he groped her, "did you know I was taking karate? I'm a brown belt."

He laughed it off but he also backed off. He still didn't realize that he'd failed, and was losing any chance with Cyn. His ego was simply too big for him to admit defeat or to realize he'd already lost.

Except for Amy, Cyn kept her suspicions to herself while her friends were there. Shortly after they'd left, she got a call from Amy.

"Just so you know," Amy said, "Tom mentioned that he didn't like David. He said he thought there was something off about David, like maybe he was trying to take advantage of you."

"I knew Tom was smart."

"Of course he's smart, he's marrying me." Amy laughed.

The next morning Cyn got up and dressed to meet with her lawyer. She made coffee and ate a small breakfast, just toast and two eggs.

She got to the law office early and greeted his receptionist Cheryl, a petite redhead who was almost scarily efficient. She sat in one of his scoop back chairs in the waiting area and turned down a cup of coffee Cheryl offered. She waited, looking around at the sleek, modern style of his office. It was funny, she realized, for all the sleek modern decor, it was warm and friendly, efficient and yet simple. There were lithographs of classic paintings on the walls, a deep blue carpet, with the walls a warm beige.

When she was shown into his office, she sat facing his large walnut desk. He kept the surface clear except for his computer, phone, pens, and some files arranged neatly in trays. Of course, he also had some pictures of his family. He had law books, most in a law library with only a few of the ones he used most often in a bookcase on one wall, and some personal mementos in another bookcase. She saw golf trophies, a collection of miniature cars, and some framed photos, including one of himself and Cyn's father on a fishing trip, and another of Cyn and her father at the Kentucky Derby with Cyn in an elaborate hat, covered in flowers.

She smiled and greeted her attorney. "Hello, Glenn, I'm back like a bad penny. How is it going with Gertrude's attempts to overturn the will and rob me of my inheritance?"

"You know her, Cyn. Gertrude is very cagey. It will be a fight, but I am sure we'll win. I have to, not just for you, but for your father. He was a great friend, as well as a major client."

"I know, he trusted you." She smiled and added, "And he considered you a friend as well."

He paused as his phone rang. "I'm sorry to bother you, Glenn," Cheryl said. "I have a call from Cyn's private investigator."

"Put him through."

"That was Lewis," he said after he hung up. "He has learned that Gertrude is indeed connected to David Fulsom." He paused. "In fact, she is his mother. He is her son from her second marriage."

"Oh, my God." Cyn was caught off guard. Whatever had made her suspicious, it was not that.

"It seems they have worked together to con and cheat people. I believe she is worse. I believe she is a murderer, and it seems he is just a con man. So far, he's shown no taste for real violence. I also know they've had several explosive fights. She's put him in the hospital a couple of times, so it's a real love-hate relationship, but when they're not fighting, they work together."

Cyn went pale. She looked as though she might faint, and she sat still, almost frozen.

"How are you doing?" he asked with genuine concern. "Cheryl," he hit his intercom, "please bring me a cola for Cyn."

"I know you're shocked," his voice was tender, "but this could very well be the evidence we need to get Gertrude arrested."

She sipped the cola and slowly relaxed. "I know, Glenn, but I feel like I'm living in a fairy tale."

"What do you mean?" he asked.

"Well, I have the wicked stepmother and two stepsisters just like Cinderella; and the seven boys remind me of the seven dwarfs as in Snow White. Of course, it's practically impossible to get Gertrude away from her mirror." She grinned. "All I'm missing is Prince Charming. I really need Prince Charming."

"Your name even fits, Cynthia Wright Snowden. Cynthia for Cinderella, and Wright Snowden for Snow White."

Cyn laughed in spite of herself. "Let's just hope it all ends with happily ever after."

"If I have anything to say about it, it will." He grinned and rose to walk her out.

She shook his hand and left, walking down the city street to find a shop for some gifts for the boys. She was distracted, her mind racing as she stood at the corner waiting for the signal to turn. She caught a whiff of cologne that unpleasantly reminded her of David, then felt a quick push on her back and fell into the path of an oncoming bus.

Chapter Three

In Shadows and Dreams

Cyn became aware of herself, her consciousness, but not of her body. She felt no pain, no fear, just a sensation as if she were floating. Soon she became aware of another presence. Someone was with her.

"Where am I?" she thought, "and who are you?"

"Ye are in what I call the land of shadows and dreams, lass." She could hear the answer in her head as if she were reading someone's mind. "And I am Robbie McDougal."

"I am Cynthia Wright Snowden but they call me Cyn. Am I dead?" she asked in her mind.

"No, lass, not yet," came the answer, the words sounding in her head once more, and this time she noted the Scottish accent. "They call ye sin? Are ye wicked?"

"Not sin like the church sees it," she laughed, "but C Y N, as in a short version of my name. Am I dying then?" She felt no fear.

"Ye may well be, I dinnae know," came the answer. "All the lasses that have been here with me have died."

"How did you come to be here?" she wondered, thinking the question.

"'Twas a spell put on me by a witch. I am to find a true love ere I can leave." The explanation floated into her mind, surprising her.

"A witch?" She was puzzled. "No one believes in witches anymore."

"Then how did you come to be here, lass?" he queried.

"I was hit by a bus," she said bluntly.

"A what? What is a bus?" He was puzzled.

"What is... how long have you been here?" She had a bit of a giggle in her mind.

"I do not know," he said softly. "Here, there is no time, only now."

"What year did you come to be here? Do you know that?" Her curiosity knew no bounds.

"'Twas in the year of our Lord 1584."

"Now it's 2017." She paused then asked, "Can we see each other?"

"Hold my hand, in your mind, lass," he instructed her. "We can see each other and get to know each other."

"And can I show you some of the changes in this time? There are things that would surprise you," she told him. "And some of them may help me survive."

"Yes, lass, but what has changed?" came the answer. "There are still men and women, lass, and they still fall in love?"

"Yes, of course, but not always men with women." She grinned. "Today, sometimes men love men and women love women. There is more to the word love that is acceptable today."

"Then 'tis no wonder this world seems strange to me." There was a pause. "And ye, lass, do ye love women?"

"No, I have never truly been in love, but I am definitely attracted to men." She was sure of that.

"'Tis good. Now hold my hand, lass, and we can see each other. You can show me a little of your world."

Cyn saw a handsome man with chiseled features and long, wavy black hair. He had blazing blue eyes. He was dressed in a strange costume. A kilt? She wondered, but even as she wondered the words breacan-an-feileadh came into her mind. He stared at her as if he had not seen a woman in well, forever. He seemed to like looking at her but then he looked down in horror and she could see what he saw: It was herself, in a hospital bed, covered in bandages and connected with all the tubes and wires of modern medicine.

"What are they doing to the puir lass? It seems they are torturing her!" He was shocked.

"That poor lass is me, and they are working to save me," she thought the explanation. "See that machine beeping? With the lines? It shows them what is happening in my heart, brain, and lungs. The tubes in my arm are giving me nutrition, medicine, and fluids, even blood."

"'Tis strange." He shook his head.

"And wondrous. Let me show you more," she offered, holding out her hand.

They walked, floated really, through the hospital. The first thing that amazed him was what people were wearing, the scrubs and lab coats of the doctors and nurses were surprising enough, but the clothes of the visitors? Men and women wearing shorts and tank tops, slacks and sweaters, it was all so strange to him, especially pants and shorts on women. He had to admit to himself that he liked women in shorts and miniskirts.

She showed him the delivery room, with a baby being born, and also in that department, a woman getting a sonogram. The picture of a baby still in the womb amazed him. They looked at the newborns. Further along, they saw someone dying even as they shocked his heart to attempt to save him. He saw the reluctance of the doctors as they pronounced the patient dead. He also saw them quickly gather themselves and go back to the next patient.

She told him about transplants, though he found that hard to believe. Then they went to the roof and she showed him a helicopter landing with a critical patient. He saw both the frantic rush and the endless waiting in the emergency room.

Looking out a window, she pointed out the traffic, including a bus. The city roads were snarled and barely moving. She told him about how traffic slowed during rush hour, which he thought was funny. Explaining speeds seemed to be hard for him to grasp. He thought a galloping horse was fast, so telling him that cars could easily double that speed astounded him. Looking up, she showed him an airplane and told him there could be more than a hundred people in it, and that it was far faster than a car.

Then, suddenly tired, she lost her connection to him and was alone once more.

The next time she became aware of her surroundings, she woke confused. She had visions or were they dreams? She felt as if she were in two different places outside the hospital room in Intensive Care. One was a crude hut, and the other a medieval castle. The people in her dreams were familiar to her but not friends, not even family, really. They were her stepmother and two stepsisters. Cyn knew that at least one of them was her deadly enemy. As she realized who she was dreaming about, she moaned softly in her head.

Her companion in the land of shadows spoke in her head.

"Lass, where are ye? Where do ye go in yer head, I mean," he asked quietly.

"I seem to go to two different places, they are like what we call fairy tales today, but filled with people I seem to know."

"We need to go to these places together. It is a way to get to know each other. To see if we fall in love," he said firmly.

"And if we do?" she asked quickly.

"I dinnae know." He seemed unsettled.

"And if we don't?" She was amused.

"I dinnae know," he admitted.

"There seems to be a lot you don't know." She laughed. "And what if I die?"

"I will be sad, alone, and waiting again. It has happened to me before," he admitted with a touch of sadness.

"Tell me, please," she requested.

"There are three I really remember. One was named Marie, and I met her in Paris during what was called the French Revolution. I did love her but they..." He trailed off.

"I know," came her sympathetic response.

"Then there was Kate, she was on a wagon train going to California when she took ill and died far short of her destination. She seemed nice and very strong-willed. The wagon train she was on was called a Donner."

"Of my goodness. I think you misunderstood, that was not a kind of wagon train, that was a very infamous wagon train. It was plagued by mishaps, bad leadership, and bad weather." She paused, sadly. "She may have been lucky to die before..."

"Before what?" He was puzzled.

"The Donner Party got stranded by a terrible snow storm. They could not find any food, some of them, well, some of them starved to death." She felt sad for Kate, doomed even if she had survived her illness. "And some ate the dead."

"I am glad she never went through that," he said sincerely.

"And the third?"

"She was what they called a flapper." He was both a little angry and amused. "She had been shot by a gangster and she was so angry, so scared, that I could not reach her."

There was regret coming through in her mind.

"Well, we have modern medicine now, but still, some live and some die. I may well die," she admitted, "but I will fight to stay alive."

"If ye die, I go back to my grave and wait," he told her. "Maybe if we get to know each other better, it might help ye live."

"I'd like to avoid dying and having you return to your grave. What can we do?" she asked.

"Take my hand and let yourself go into one of the places in yer dreams. I will be with ye and see what happens," he suggested.

"All right, Robbie, I will." She drifted off.

Chapter Four

Cinderella

Cynthia woke up in a strange place. She had a fierce headache, and she also felt tired and disoriented. She ached all over. She looked around, puzzled, wondering where she was, but she couldn't help noticing that her surroundings were strangely primitive. Her strongest memories were of a very different place. She remembered a large, modern city filled with people bustling around, noisy traffic and tall buildings. She also remembered living on a sprawling horse ranch with soft green hills and white fences. There were beautiful horses, including some mares with frisky foals. The ranch also had a tennis court and a pool. She also remembered several boys, seven of them. Were they all her brothers? She knew she loved them. She felt the grief of a recent loss, in fact, her sharpest memory was of the shock and grief she felt over her father's sudden death. There were two older stepsisters she sometimes loved and sometimes barely tolerated. She even remembered a stepmother she detested with every fiber of her being.

She also had a vague memory of a place entirely strange. A castle? She tried to focus her mind on the here and now she found herself in. As she looked at her surroundings, she wondered where she was, even wondered when she was. She soon realized she was lying on something really rough and lumpy, and very scratchy.

She realized it was a crude mattress on a crude pallet atop a dirt floor. The rough mattress seemed to be filled with straw. No wonder she ached in every bone. She had a thin blanket made of crude, coarse fabric and no pillow. She found herself in a cramped room that seemed to be a storage room, at least it was full of strange things. She stood up slowly and with one hand rubbed her back as she looked around at her surroundings. The room was in a rough wooden building. She thought it was some kind of wooden hut or shed. It was dirty and as she continued to look around, she noted it was strangely primitive, barely worthy of the name cottage.

As she continued to take in her surroundings, she was surprised to learn that it was more of a house than a hut. There was a set of rickety stairs near the fireplace. She thought about going up the stairs but the sound of someone snoring coming faintly from above warned her to stay downstairs. She feared who might be up those stairs.

The rest of the downstairs included a small living area and a cooking area, with a wobbly table and three chairs. It seemed strangely crude. Stretching again and still rubbing the small of her back, she walked to the door, opened it, and looked out.

She could see a barren yard.

Across the yard, there was a crude barn, a small pen with a wooden watering trough, a small garden overgrown with weeds and looking to be in serious need of watering. The pen had a few scrawny goats, three unshorn sheep, and two lazy pigs. All of the animals looked far too skinny. Chickens roamed around the yard pecking hopefully at the bare dirt. The garden seemed to be planted with vegetables but not much was worth eating. The barn looked as if it might crumble at any moment.

She used her fingers to smooth out her long, black hair and found a small string to tie it back in a tail. She smoothed her rough beige dress and found an equally rough brown apron to tie over it, around her slender waist. She slid her feet into poorly made leather sandals. Following instinct, she walked out the door and went into the barn. She sighed as she stepped into the small barn, a shed really because she knew in her gut she had work waiting inside, hard work.

Once in the barn, she found two skinny cows with their bags full, mooing loudly, and an old bay mare, who looked as if she may once have been a beautiful creature. Knowing instinctively she was responsible for these animals, she set to work. She found enough hay, even a bit of grain, to feed the horse and the cows.

Carrying a bucket out to the trough she got water for all three animals. She found a stool and pulled it over to sit on so she could milk the cows, hoping they were placid. Then she sat on the stool and began to milk one of the cows. The animal was restless, not kicking at Cinderella, but moving quite a bit, and swishing her tail. She sang softly while she worked, calming her. The other cow was passive, concentrating on her meager portion of hay. She was glad that the cows were both gentle animals. When she was done, she set aside the bucket of milk. Next, she fed and watered the sheep, pigs, and goats. She realized one of the goats also needed to be milked, so she did. Once that chore was finished, she tossed some grain to the chickens and hunted around, managing to find a few eggs.

She was about to water the garden when she heard a familiar screech.

"Cinderella!" She knew it was her stepmother's voice. "Cinderella! Get in here and fix our breakfasts. Your sisters and I are hungry!"

It was a terrible shock to be called Cinderella, a name she vaguely remembered from a childish fairy tale. Deep inside, somehow, she had known. She quickly tried to recall the details of the story, but all she could remember was Cinderella doing endless chores and being harped at by her stepmother and two stepsisters. She had the impression that the maiden was a wimp who let her demanding stepmother and the two spoiled brats, the stepsisters, order her around, without doing any of the work themselves. They treated her as a slave. Cynthia snorted as she thought that. As soon as she was called Cinderella, her memories of any other life began to fade, however, there was still enough

Cynthia Snowden in her to stand up for herself. Things in this fairy tale were going to change! This Cinderella was no slave, and damn it, she was certainly not a wimp!

Still, she felt her inner strength and resolve beginning to fade as she heard Gertrude call out again, "Cinderella! Get in here. We are starving. You need to fix our morning meal and then we have a long list of chores for you to do while we go into town."

"Gertrude, you shrieked?" Cinderella asked calmly as she entered the cottage. "If you are hungry you can fix yourself some food. If you have things that need to get done, do them. I am not your servant and never will be."

Cinderella sat down the two buckets of milk, emptied the eggs out of her deep pockets, and looked around for a place to sit down, finding only three chairs. She stared at them, understanding that there was not one for her. She was not supposed to sit, ever.

"You will do as you are told, girl, or we will beat you," Gertrude sneered.

Cinderella walked right up to Gertrude, looked her straight in the eyes and said two words, "Try it."

"What did you say to me?" Gertrude was shocked.

"You would beat me?" Cinderella smiled dangerously. "You could only try, at your own peril."

"Are you threatening me girl?" Gertrude tried but she could not hide her shock.

"No, Gertrude," Cinderella said calmly, "I am responding to your threat. One which you should well regret making."

Gertrude stared at Cinderella, reading her face. Something in her eyes shook Gertrude. She staggered a few steps back. "What do you mean?"

"All those chores you have me doing?" Cinderella's smile was deadly. "They made me strong. All that sitting around on your fat bottoms you and your daughters do? They make you weak."

"Ladies, real ladies, do not need strength," Gertrude said in a stuffy tone. "We are not men. We are more fragile and delicate, that is why we have men to protect us."

"What men are there here, in this hovel, to protect you, Gertrude?" Cinderella sneered. "I've seen none. You act and dress as if you are a great lady. You put on airs, but there are no men courting you or either of your daughters."

"And who courts you?" Gertrude shot back with a well-aimed barb. "You dress in rags and smell like horse droppings. Now fix our meal or I will find a way to have you tossed out, I vow it."

"Toss me out? So what? Being away from the likes of you would be a pleasure," Cinderella countered. "And who would you have doing your chores and cooking your food without me? Bridget?"

Bridget gasped, worried, as she slapped a hand to her thin, flat chest. She was horrified and all too aware that the threat was very real. She had never stood up to her mother and her sister Bianca.

Ignoring her, Gertrude sneered, "I still have friends in court, even the king respects our family name. I can accuse you of theft and have you imprisoned. It may even be true, your father's fortune is missing. Since his death we have nothing."

Cinderella felt a stab of pain at the mention of her father's death. She had already known in her heart he was gone, he would never have left her such dire circumstances. Moreover, she was instinctively suspicious of her father's death in any reality.

Gertrude's brown eyes took on a feverish glow of true madness. "In fact, I can accuse you of murdering your father. Someone killed him, mayhaps I can say it was you. Be careful, Cinderella. I know I can make them think 'tis true."

Cinderella had a moment of clarity. "You are pure evil. I will find a way to prove it and then we will see how you like prison or even the chopping block."

"You cannot prove anything if we throw you out, wench, so you remain with us and spy on us. You can search in vain for proof of the truth of your father's death and try to locate his fortune, and you will find naught. I am far too clever for the likes of you." In spite of her harsh words, Gertrude had a touch of fear in her voice. "If you wish to stay with us, you will do the chores we have for you, starting with our morning meal. We will give you a list of chores for today after we eat."

"I will not be a slave to you and your lazy daughters," Cinderella shouted.

"I will go to the king," Gertrude started.

"The king only respects our family name because he was a true friend to my father," Cinderella interrupted, her voice was soft and deadly. "He knows me, as a child perhaps, but he does know me. He does not know you. My influence is surely as great with him as yours."

Gertrude wanted to scream in frustration. She knew well how clever Cinderella was, she was brighter and quicker than her own daughters, and much more beautiful. There was a possibility, small but real, that Cinderella could prove how her father had died. Soon, she thought, I may have to make sure she follows her father to the grave. As soon as I find the fortune her father had hidden away. She was sure Cinderella knew where it was, and that was the only thing keeping her alive.

Cinderella silently decided to pretend obedience to Gertrude and her daughters. She tamped down her rebellious nature and decided to find out the truth of her father's death. Then she would bring Gertrude and the girls down, all the way down.

"As I said, take care Cinderella!" There was a touch of fear behind the anger in Gertrude's voice.

"I will find a way to prove you are behind my father's death," Cinderella threatened, and it was no empty threat, she meant every word.

Cinderella quickly threw together a crude meal: bread and butter, a minuscule portion of bacon and an egg for each woman. She sliced a potato and let it fry in the grease from the bacon. She very deliberately burned the eggs and left the bacon just a bit rare. She cooked the whole meal without the use of any seasonings.

When she started to sit at the table, Gertrude yelled out, "Wench, you would dare sit and eat with us? Go back to your chores!"

Cinderella quickly complied, although she put on an air of rebellion. She knew full well the crude meal was inedible. When the three women left, she would have a well-cooked meal.

Cinderella began with her most hated chore, carrying the chamber pots out from the bedrooms. It took her three trips as she carried the smelly pots right past the breakfast table, earning a protest from all three women. She was smiling as she sat the pots at the edge of the clearing. She began sweeping the cottage next, beginning by the kitchen, if that room deserved the title. The cottage only had a dirt floor, but she swept it daily, sweeping all the loose dirt and dust out the door, again right past the women who were still eating.

Disgusted and choking from the dust, the three women quickly finished the meager meal. Bianca and Bridget both went to their bedrooms to ready themselves for the trip to town.

Gertrude stayed back to list Cinderella's chores for the day. "First you will harness the mare to the carriage for our trip to town before you clean the cottage, the kitchen, of course, and there is laundry for all three of us that needs to be done. Bianca and I also have some mending for you. I left mine on the bed. All three of us need our rooms to be cleaned, swept and dusted. We need fresh bedding and the bedding you are changing out needs to be washed. If all of that isn't done and done right by the time we return I will take a switch to your lazy backside. Do you understand me?" Gertrude's smug superiority was shaky and Cinderella knew it.

"No, Gertrude." Cinderella was furious. "You will understand me. You will never beat me again! I will not allow it. Your switch can be used on yourself. Do you doubt me? Also, remember there are things I know, things that can leave you in jeopardy, things that can put you in a dungeon. Do you understand me?"

"I do not believe you, lying slut!" Gertrude was so angry her double chins shook and her large sagging breasts heaved.

"Try me, Gertrude, if you dare." Her voice was low, and that was somehow more threatening. "And Gertrude? If you call me out as a slut, I have a good defense. I am a virgin."

"That can be changed," Gertrude sneered.

"Not by you!" Cinderella retorted with a snort.

"I know men who would gladly steal your virginity from you, and make it very painful, mayhaps even deadly." Gertrude left the cottage, leaving Cinderella stunned and shaking in her wake.

Cynthia's stepsisters came out of their chambers. As usual, they were overdressed in beads, feathers, and laces. The colors each wore were wrong for their skin tones. Bridget looked flushed, and Bianca looked sallow and pale. It was ridiculous, Cinderella thought, Gertrude simply could not stand to have any woman near her who looked good, and so she gave her own daughters bad advice on their clothing.

As the daughters hurried to catch up with their mother Bridget gave Cinderella a shy smile.

"Have a good day, Cinderella," she said quietly. "Do not work too hard."

Cinderella stood there for a moment, quieting her nerves before she took advantage of the peace and cooked herself a well-made meal. The bacon was perfectly cooked and seasoned, her egg fluffy, the bread warm, soft, and covered with butter and honey.

Once she had eaten, she quickly cleaned the dishes. She knew she had to begin the chores. Pretending to be obedient to Gertrude's orders was hard work. She knew she had a long list of chores to do, and she was fully aware of how miserable Gertrude would make her life if they were not done when the women returned, so she set to work.

She quickly cleaned the three bedchambers, pulling all the bedding in the bedrooms, balling it up. She carried the soiled bed sheets and clothing down the stairs and set it all just outside the door. Next, she straightened and dusted the rooms. She pulled the mending Gertrude had left on her bed and found the things Blanche wanted to be mended and set it all on the crude table. She turned to the laundry next, washing everything rather defiantly in the trough, before refilling it with clean water. She hung the wet garments wherever she could, on bushes, and even from the hut's roof. She used a brush to clean off dirt from the things that could not be washed and to beat the one small rug.

She cleaned and dusted the… what would you call it, she wondered, the living room? She also cleaned the kitchen and cooking area, making sure there was plenty of firewood for the next day.

She gathered the chamber pots and the bucket of ashes from the stove to empty them off the bluff. Once she tossed the contents off the bluff, there was no putting it off, she drew a deep breath and rinsed the chamber pots, using rough sand to scrub them. That done, she put them back in the house and smiled.

Her chores were finally done, at least until the women returned. Of course, she still had evening chores, including caring for the animals, but still she felt a sense of achievement at the completed work. She decided to take advantage of her freedom and climb the hill to the pond for a swim.

That was when her day went from bad to worse.

"Why does she let them treat her like that? Like servant or a slave. I never realized Cinderella was such a wimp," Cyn thought angrily.

"What is a wimp?" Robbie asked.

"Someone who is too weak or scared to stand up for herself, or himself." Her answer was clear.

"I think you are wrong," Robbie replied. "She is trying to stand up

for herself but she is too caring to let the animals suffer. She also seems to want to find out the truth about her father's death. Part of her weakness is a sham, a way to spy on the wicked Gertrude and the truly weak sisters."

"You're right, but it's very maddening," Cyn conceded.

"Yes, it is." She felt his grin. "Let us continue the story."

Chapter Five

Cinderella

Cinderella, as she always did, had climbed the hill and thrown the ashes and waste off the bluff a short distance from her house. It was something she did without thought, something she did every day, something she thoroughly hated having to do. She closed her mind and strove to close off her sense of smell. She just blindly threw the contents of the pots into the breeze off the cliff. There were several things happening that day that Cinderella didn't know. How could she know?

How could she know that today would be different? That today, doing the detested chore, would lead to personal disaster? To a fateful meeting that could deflect her anger towards her family and even change her life? How could she know that anyone was riding along the road just below the steep bluff?

She certainly didn't know that the cliff she emptied the buckets from was within range of the road far below when the wind conditions were just right. And how could she know that of all the people who might be riding there as she emptied out the waste and ashes, it would be young Prince Robert out riding on his great warhorse? How could she know that he was in a fierce mood already?

She did not know that the Prince and two of his guards ever rode along that road, let alone that they were there that very day. She did not know that the Prince had a notoriously quick temper, especially when he felt slighted in front of any of his men. And she certainly did not know that some of the ashes and even a few drops of the other waste had landed on him. Nothing that happened that day was her fault in any way. She just wanted to get to the pond in time for her swim before she had to return to start the evening chores.

Humming to herself, she followed the path and the stream down to a small, clear pond, surrounded by lush grass and shaded by tall leafy trees. Looking around quickly, she could see no one. She quickly disrobed, hung her grubby dress on a nearby branch, pulled off her shift and hung it next to her dress, and leapt into the pond. The water felt cool and wonderful on her naked skin. Her long black hair flowed in the water as she floated on her back, relaxing. She felt so relaxed and free. She began to swim lazily. Swimming was only one of the many pleasures Cinderella's stepmother, Gertrude, denied her. The denial was not from any concern or love of Cinderella but from fear that if Cinderella were to drown, she and her two daughters would actually have to do the chores themselves.

Still, it seemed that the world was so beautiful and peaceful that she felt she could truly relax and enjoy the pleasant interlude.

She was wrong. Very, very wrong.

So Cinderella swam, relaxed and tranquil, not knowing that her idyll was about to come to an abrupt and painful end.

It so happened that it was a terrible day for Cinderella's carelessness. The Prince was already in a bad mood before ever having the ashes blown into his face. The ashes escalated his bad mood into outright anger when he felt the first droplets hit his velvet riding coat. He had looked up in time to see the chamber pot being emptied. The anger turned into a white-hot fury. He quickly kicked his great black warhorse into a gallop to get away from the foul mess but in truth, not many drops could have reached him even if he had stood his ground. He was really quite far from the person emptying the waste.

Angered, the young Prince rode quickly to find out who had committed such an insult to his royal person. He was not usually an unjust or unreasonable man, but on this day he was in a foul mood. His father, King Nigel, and his mother, Queen Dorothea, were demanding that he marry, and he was not yet ready to give up his freedom for the chains of a wife and children, or for the added responsibilities of the kingdom his father wanted him to assume. Did they not realize that he was still young? Barely twenty? There were still too many tankards of ale to drink, and very many maids to tumble before he married and began a family. He wanted what his parents had, a marriage built on love, respect, and faithfulness, but he was not yet ready to give up the pleasures of youth.

The only reason he was out riding at all that day was to escape his royal mother's nagging tongue. He dearly loved the woman but he had to admit, she could bring a saint to his knees with the rough side of her tongue. She was utterly relentless! He had ridden hard to escape the guards who were assigned to ride with him even though he counted them as friends, for he dearly wanted some time to himself, even a few timeless moments. However, even that was denied him, for his guards were close by. They were friends, true and loyal to the Prince, but they answered to the King and Queen.

He wanted to soothe his temper with some peace and quiet, and some rare, precious solitude. He understood his parents' concern. He was the only Prince and his parents wanted him to marry and produce heirs to the throne while they were still alive.

Part of the problem was that they had even picked out a suitable match for him. By all criteria, she was perfect to wed him. The woman they sought to have him marry was a princess from a nearby kingdom. A marriage between the two of them would unite the two kingdoms, bringing more wealth into his own realm. It would be a good match for defense reasons as well. There was only one thing holding the prince back from his responsibilities and agreeing to the match. He had met with the woman when she traveled to his home for a visit and he simply did not like her. She was older than he was, at three and twenty, and very plain. He could have overlooked that and agreed to the match but he found her manners crude and her attitude demanding. The match would be good for the kingdom but not for the prince.

Another thing that riled him so much was their unspoken fear that if he were to meet an untimely end without issue, they would have no one to succeed themselves as King and Queen, and the kingdom would pass away from their family. It was vaguely unsettling to realize that his parents feared for his mortality. The fact that they feared out of concern for the kingdom instead of their love for him only chafed him even more. If he had not been so irked by his mother's nagging he would have admitted to himself that he knew they did, indeed, worry for him out of love, as any parents worry for their child. On this day, however, he was too irritated and upset to think rationally. And that was before he was hit with the ashes and the contents of the chamber pot.

His smoldering temper burst into full flame as he sought out the villain who had covered him with ashes and piss, especially since the ashes were making him sneeze. Sneezing always made the young Prince feel so undignified and common.

It was a long sweeping path around the bluffs to the point where the ashes and disgusting waste had come from. It was also too narrow and steep to safely travel at a full gallop. Even though he hurried, it took him almost a quarter hour to reach the top of the bluff. By the time the Prince found the tiny wood and stone cottage tucked away in the overgrown woods, there was no one to be seen.

Cinderella had finished her chores for the moment, and she knew she was doing something wild and wicked. Something just a little daring. She was swimming naked in the pond, really relaxing for the first time in days. There she was alone, free and, for once, no one was yelling at her.

That is no one yelled at her until the Prince came upon her and asked if she knew who the fool was that was throwing all kinds of foul matter on the future King. She hunched down under the water and looked up into angry green eyes and defiantly told him that if he got filth all over his royal self, it was his own royal fault.

It was unfortunate for her that she was naked. Unfortunate that she was feeling defiant, that she was not in a mood to let herself be yelled at by anybody, royal Prince or not, no matter how handsome he was. Unfortunate that the Prince was in one of his very rare foul moods. Such a foul mood that he barely noticed her beauty. He barely noticed the delicacy of her features. He paid no attention to the creamy softness of her skin. He never saw the full thrust of her bare breasts as he rode his horse right into the pond and reached down to pull the furiously struggling, naked girl out of the water.

He lifted her up and dragged her across his horse's back. He placed her so that she was draped across the hard cantle of his saddle; her head was hanging down by the foreleg of his great warhorse, and the ends of her long hair were flowing in the water.

She was off balance; her bottom was straight up in the air and she was draped too far over the horse's withers to stay in place without the prince holding her firmly in position. The feel of the hard saddle beneath her was very uncomfortable.

She was furious, indignant and terrified.

In spite of her struggling and wiggling, her attempts to slap and kick at him, he managed to control her quite easily. She managed to give his hand a quick, hard bite but the hand was encased in his glove. Holding her in place with one large hand, he spanked her bare bottom with the other. It was a long, harsh spanking. His hand rose and fell in a relentless rhythm. The heavy black leather riding glove he wore made a loud smacking sound as it landed on her wet butt, and each blow really stung. He alternated cheeks but landed the blows on the same area of each cheek. The pain of those two large, bright red spots was intense. This was not a playful romp; it was a real spanking meant to punish, and punish it did.

He was so involved in spanking her that he never heard his two guards ride up. He never heard their laughter, but she did. It added to her anger and humiliation.

He just continued spanking her. He didn't leave her with any bruises but he did cause her bottom to turn bright red and flaming hot. Because the heavy gloves protected his hands, he was hitting her even harder than he realized. She was very red and had two large splotches, one on each cheek. Finally, he stopped.

He held her for a moment while she continued to struggle. She was conscious of her flaming, aching bottom and also of the discomfort from her position on the horse. She felt the rough texture of the horse's mane, the boniness of his withers, along with the hard leather of the cantle of the prince's saddle, and the rough cloth of his breeches. She even felt the rigid bulge under that cloth. Finally, wisely, she quieted.

Disdainfully, he dropped her back into the shockingly cool water. He glanced at her as she shivered with the jolt of cold water on her flaming butt and realized that she was indeed, a very comely maid. She had a firm body with perfect skin and full thrusting breasts. They looked even larger and more luscious because she was heaving with anger. The nipples were tipped with a dusky rose tint and tightened by the cold water into tight little buds.

Seeing his gaze, she turned her back to him. Her long wet hair was streaming over her soft shoulders. She had a tiny waist, gently flared hips, and round firm buttocks, now turned dark red, with purple bruises beginning to form in the center of each cheek. She looked up over her shoulder at him with bright blue eyes, shiny with tears she struggled to hold back. Her defiance and outrage were barely held in check.

In spite of her anger, she felt a thrill course through her veins at the sight of the young Prince. He was quite possibly the most handsome man she had ever seen. His black hair was pulled back into a queue and his brilliant green eyes flared with an unnamed emotion. He was wearing a black velvet riding coat trimmed with gold braid and had on a green vest. His shirt was pure white linen with a froth of lace at the collar and cuffs. He was wearing snug, russet breeches and, against her will, her vision was drawn to the bulge of his manhood straining against the tightness of his crotch.

They both stood there, silent and still, for a long moment before he reached down and once again dragged her out of the water. He pulled her into his arms and kissed her. It was no tender, tentative, gentle first kiss like a gentleman should give an innocent maid. It was not a lover's kiss, tender but coaxing ever more passion. It was an insulting and demanding kiss with thrusting tongue and hard, intense lips. The passion in it was full blown and instantaneous.

She struggled briefly before succumbing to the passion and ardor of the kiss. Her senses were filled with him. His hand started to slide towards her breast, capturing it. He gently stroked her nipple while he continued to kiss her. The kiss seemed to go on forever before the Prince heard someone calling his name. It was one of his guards! The man was laughing!

"Your Highness, do you want us to lose ourselves again?" the older guard asked. "Or should we drag this creature back to the castle for you?"

The Prince broke off the kiss abruptly, barely avoiding her slap. "What? What would I want with her at the castle?"

"Well, when we first saw you with her you seemed to be intent on beating her black and blue," the guard said slowly. "Did she mayhaps commit some insult on your royal person? We could have her beheaded if you wish."

"He dinnae look to me like he wanted her beheaded," the other, younger guard grinned. "He looked like he just wanted her bedded."

"The Prince interested in a girl?" the first guard jested. "'Tis

49

the Queen who would want the girl at the palace."

"The Queen wants to see me married. Preferably in love and married, but love or not, married." The Prince said softly, "She knows I oft bed the lasses, but she wants to see me tied to just one and producing heirs."

"So if this girl has caught your eye," the first guard said with an open grin, "the Queen would want to know about it. In the space of a heartbeat, she would have a priest ready to join you to the lass, whoever she is."

"Even the Queen wants to be sure the girl I wed is worthy," the Prince said. "Not a common strumpet such as this."

He stole another passionate kiss and avoided another attempted slap before dropping her into the cool water once again. Without a word, he kicked his horse and rode off in a splash of water followed by a cloud of dust.

He left behind an intrigued and angry woman. A woman who had been pushed around far too many times, threatened far too many times, and who worked far too hard. Now, her anger and frustration at all the wrongs in her life had a focus. The Prince. She was hell-bent on seeing him again. For revenge, she told herself.

Only for revenge.

"Oh my goodness, he looks just like you!" Shocked and shaken, she let go of his hand. "And he really spanked the hell out of her, or me, whoever. Do you treat women like that?"

"No, lass, I might play with a woman, but I have never hurt one." He smiled and took her hand. "In God's truth, never."

"The strange thing is, even with how he treated her, she is attracted to him." Cyn was puzzled.

"Women are strange and wondrous creatures." He laughed.

Chapter Six

Cinderella

Although he was unaware of it, there was a loving plot being planned against the Prince. The day before the Prince left the castle in a rare temper, the King and Queen had a discussion. Truth be told, they were not any more pleased with the foreign princess than the Prince was himself.

The King paced around the bedchamber while the Queen sat at a small table, outlining her plan. She knew she had to convince two stubborn men, her husband, the King, and her son.

"We do not need to insist he marry the princess. In truth, I do not like her very much and I was hoping to have a small degree of affection for the mother of my grandchildren. She is not attractive or overly bright, and her manners are horrible! She is rude, demanding, and cares for no one but herself," she said as she stood up and followed him. She placed her small hand on his shoulder. "Our marriage was arranged for us but we were pleased with each other, even at our first meeting. I saw you, so handsome, with your dark hair and your blue eyes that seemed to glow and I was infatuated with you, but it was not your looks I fell in love with, it was the kind, decent man you are. Indeed, after all these years we are still in love and we are happy with each other, are we not?"

"Yes, we are. Then what is your plan, my lady?" The King smiled because he knew well his wife and he could see that she had something in mind.

"We push him to marry the princess as we have been. His sense of duty will be at war with his dislike for the princess, then as a major concession to ensure his happiness," she smiled widely, "we tell him the choice is his. We offer to throw a royal ball and invite any eligible maid we can find. He will be so pleased to have a choice, instead of the princess, he may well pick someone we could approve of as a wife."

"And if his choice is unworthy?" the King asked quietly.

"He may well choose someone to bed that we would not accept. I am sure he beds his share of the women around here." She looked at her husband and smiled. "As I know you did before we met. However, in the matter of a wife, I trust his common sense. Do you?"

"I do, and so we invite not only the high born maids, but all young maidens." The King arched an eyebrow. "We make the choice seem to be truly his, whilst we aim the more worthy women towards him. Let us send out a proclamation now. We will also send messengers to other realms."

"When will we hold this event?" she asked, still smiling.

"One month, Milady," he said gently. "It will be the same month as that in which you were introduced to me as my future wife. I remember it well. You seemed startled and confused. You went out to wander in the garden for a short time. I went to search you out and found you in the center of the maze, and we fell in love, right there." The King kissed her with some heat. "We first made love there."

"I remember well, making love in the maze, and now I know the legend surrounding it is true." The Queen smiled at the memory. "We must post guards to keep unworthy maidens out. Ready the proclamations, Milford, and be prepared for chaos. The staff will be hard pressed to get everything ready in that short time."

"After I send out messengers with the proclamation, my Queen," he kissed her softly, "I would like to take a long walk in the maze."

Unfortunately for Cinderella, the King and Queen waited until the next day, when the Prince returned from his ride to tell him about the ball. The Prince was still not looking forward to marriage, he felt he was too young to be wed, yet he was relieved not to have the princess forced on him. He also liked the dancing and feasting of royal balls. He found himself hoping that he might meet a worthy maiden there. Worthy of either a quick tumble or a very lengthy courtship, but not necessarily worthy of marriage.

Cinderella was storming as she dressed to go back to the hut. Still, under her rage was a current of excitement. The Prince was mesmerizing, even though she told herself she hated him. It was only another factor in her growing confusion. She remembered Cynthia Snowden's life less and less while she felt more like Cinderella. There was even a vague hint of something or someone else, nagging at a corner of her mind.

She began to stalk back to the hut but soon stopped and sat on a log, contemplating her turbulent emotions and the life she found herself trapped in. Because she stopped, she found herself late returning to the hut. When she got back to the hut Cinderella was dismayed to see the carriage standing in the yard. As usual, the three women had merely gotten out of the carriage and no one had bothered to unhitch or tend to the aging mare. She was upset to find her stepmother and stepsisters had returned home before her. She decided it was but another sin to put on the head of the Prince.

The three women were inside, chattering, full of excitement and joy instead of the anger Cinderella had expected. As Cinderella approached, however, the mood changed, the excited chatter stopped abruptly.

"Cinderella! Did you complete your chores, strumpet? You had best have done them all, else I will take a switch to your lazy backside!" Gertrude shouted, her bad temper showing through her excitement.

Cinderella was in no mood for Gertrude's orders and certainly in no mood for any threat to her already sore backside.

It ended now!

"You will never threaten me again, Gertrude, you witch!" She wondered at the flash of shock on Gertrude's face as she spoke in a firm voice. "I will do some chores and I will care for the animals but you and your daughters will care for your own rooms and your own things. You will learn to cook your own meals. I am not a servant or a slave. There will be no more threats. I wager I could best you in any fight, Gertrude, and you know it."

"My beloved daughters would support me in a fight," Gertrude shot back, although she was shocked by Cinderella's declaration. "You cannot defeat all three of us."

"Yes, three grown women against one girl. You might win but you would all be bloodied in the battle," she said with a calm, steady voice. "I promise you that."

Gertrude dropped the threats, knowing full well Cinderella meant every word. Mayhaps it was time for the worthless chit to have an accident, a fatal accident. Past time.

"Well then, girl, fix our dinner, we are exceedingly hungry," she said simply.

"I will fix dinner as soon as I tend to the mare that you just left standing in the yard. When I am ready to prepare the meal, one of you must come in and help me. You need to have someone who can help me cook," Cinderella replied, truly relieved that she seemed to have won that argument, although she was suspicious that Gertrude gave in so easily. Cinderella was no fool, she sensed she was in danger.

"Forget the damned mare. Our needs are more important. We need to eat and we have plans to discuss," Gertrude ordered.

"No, the mare comes first. The rest of the animals also need to be fed, and-" She stopped as she heard the cows mooing loudly. "The cows must be milked."

"Make haste then." For some reason, Gertrude backed down. "We are hungry and we need to speak with you."

Cinderella took care of the evening chores, quickly, not to

please the women but simply because she was hungry as well.

When she had finished caring for the animals, she came in and cooked a simple meal, with Bridget helping her. With Bridget's help, the simple meal took twice as long to prepare. Defiantly, she joined the women at the table. For once, they were too excited to complain about her sitting with them. It seemed they had wondrous news. There was going to be a royal ball! The reason behind it was even more exciting, the King and Queen wanted to find a wife for Prince Robert. The extremely handsome and very rich Prince Robert.

"The proclamation was for every unmarried maiden to come." Bridget gushed, "A royal ball at the castle. 'Tis exciting."

"Mayhaps I will catch the eye of the Prince," Bianca said, in an uncharacteristic dream voice.

Her tone amused Cinderella. "Do you really think the Prince will want you for a wife? Or you Bridget?"

"Do you not dream of marrying Prince Robert?" Bridget asked Cinderella.

"She will not be attending the ball!" Gertrude shouted. "I swear it."

Cinderella kept quiet, it was no more than she expected.

Gertrude spoke up again, "We must return to town tomorrow and buy fabric for new gowns. We need lace and trim as well."

"There is no money for fabric and trim for new gowns, Gertrude," Cinderella pointed out. "Look at this hovel. Truly look. We are poor."

"We will have to sell some things. We can sell milk, cheese, eggs and some vegetables. We can also part with a few sheep and one of the cows," Gertrude decided.

"We need the money we get for our produce and milk to buy more seed for next year. If we do not save for planting, we will have no food next harvest," Cinderella argued. "You would buy gowns now, only to starve in the winter?"

"Nevertheless, we go to town on the morrow." Gertrude stood up. "I will find a way to obtain funds for the three gowns. I have my methods." She turned towards the stairs.

"Three gowns, not four, Gertrude?" Cinderella's tone stopped the older woman in her tracks.

"As I said, you will not attend the ball." Gertrude never even turned back as she spoke to Cinderella.

"I will attend the ball else who do you think will sew these gowns for you and your daughters?" Cinderella asked quietly.

"You will, of course." Gertrude was certain as if she never expected Cinderella to ask the question.

"I will only make the gowns if I get one as well," Cinderella said with absolute conviction in her voice. "I will also attend the ball with you."

"You will not!" Gertrude could not believe her ears. She turned back to face Cinderella.

Gertrude knew well that next to Cinderella her daughters were plain. Bianca was heavy and had a strident, unpleasant voice. Bridget was thin and shy, with no skill at attracting men. She had confidence in her own charms, but her daughters were useless at finding rich husbands, indeed, she thought, they would be lucky to find any husbands at all. She wanted them each to find a husband who had funds enough to keep her daughters and herself in style.

Secretly, Gertrude had a daring plot. She knew some ways to blind a man to her age, to bind a man to her charms, at least long enough to ensnare a man into marriage. Of course, after she married the Prince, she would have to make sure the King and Queen had a tragic accident. Soon after the marriage, the Prince himself would follow his parents to the grave. In her vanity, Gertrude was oblivious to the failure of her plot against Cinderella's father, a failure that left him in a grave and herself and her daughters living in poverty. In her head that failure was not her fault. In her twisted mind, Cinderella was to blame.

"You will go with us on the morrow to town to choose the fabrics for our gowns," Gertrude commanded.

"Only if I get to choose fabric for my gown as well," Cinderella countered.

"You will," Gertrude said resentfully, ignoring a protest from Bianca.

The next day, Gertrude disappeared for a long time, leaving the girls to shop on their own. Cinderella was suspicious, wondering where Gertrude had gone. As the two older women oohed and ahhed over fabrics for the gowns, Cinderella walked over to Bridget. She was ecstatic over a bright pink silk which did not suit her coloring at all and Cinderella steered her to a pale yellow that made her skin glow. They selected lace, feathers, and trims for their gowns before Gertrude rejoined them, carrying a small bag which she seemed to hide from her daughters. She quickly picked out what she wanted for her gown. When Gertrude paid the merchant, as Cinderella feared, there was not enough money for a fourth, and the fabric for her gown was put back.

Cinderella no longer did all the chores. She tended the animals and the garden, did most of the cooking and worked on the gowns but that was all. She no longer swept or cleaned the rooms, so they went mainly unattended. She did, however, wait until Gertrude and the girls were out, visiting friends, to look in Gertrude's room. She found the small bag Gertrude had brought from town. In it, she found some candles and a vial of a strange liquid. It smelled terrible. She tasted a bit of it, and it was horrible. Some instinct had her pouring out almost all of the contents and refilling the vial with dirty water.

Ignoring Gertrude's anger, she began taking some time every few days for herself. She walked or rode the mare, looking for the Prince. When she found him, she put her plans for revenge into effect. Her goal was irritating him and causing him quite a bit of embarrassment, but no real harm. On one occasion she took his clothes while he swam, leaving him naked and bellowing when he got out. His guards gave him a cloak to wear as he rode back to the castle. The two guards wisely kept their faces solemn, with no sign of the laughter they were holding inside.

Once the Prince had gone into the castle, they doubled over in laughter. "Did you see his face?"

The younger guard nodded, still laughing, before he managed, "Do you know what happened to his clothing?"

"'Twas the girl from the pond," the older guard said. "I could have stopped her, but she deserved to get some revenge, and it was harmless."

Another time, as he again went swimming, she put a small snake, not poisonous, into his boot. The guards saw her and grinned. Watching the lass get revenge on the Prince was a very pleasant diversion as long as no real harm came of it. He truly considered the Prince to be a friend. When the Prince went to slide the boot on he gave a startled shout and pulled the wiggling serpent out, tossing it on the ground.

"How did that snake get into my boot?" he shouted, shaking out his other boot to be sure it held no serpent.

"'Twas the girl," the older guard told him.

"What girl?" He was already certain he knew well which girl.

"The one you spanked," the guard replied. "It seems she is bent on revenge."

"And you did nothing to stop the lass?" He was incredulous.

"She did not deserve the way you treated her." This guard had been with him a long time and felt free to speak his mind. "If she did aught to harm you, I would have stopped her, but these petty acts of revenge were no more than you deserved and you well know it."

The Prince was irritated but he admitted to himself that his guard was right. He had been unfair to the lass.

The third prank she pulled, however, was more serious. As the Prince and his men sat under a tree and ate a meal, she placed a burr under his stallion's saddle. The guards stopped her immediately, dragging her over to the Prince. He took her arm and forced her over as he sat on a fallen log and pulled her over his lap. This time he spanked her without the leather gloves, and without baring her bottom. He controlled his temper but he still gave her a good, long, hard spanking. He only stopped when he caught the guards laughing, and looked over to see his stallion mounting her aged mare.

Cinderella did not find him riding out again. She was too busy working on the gowns for Gertrude and her daughters. The Prince was too busy ordering and controlling the preparations for the ball.

The whole town was preparing for the event. Shops were stocked with more goods than usual. Merchants raised prices even as they were joyfully plotting in their heads on how to exploit at the extra business to make the most coin. Windows were washed and polished, as were storefronts. Some were even painted. Streets were cleaned, and flowers appeared around the village.

At the castle, everything was being polished and cleaned to gleaming perfection. Musicians were practicing constantly, filling the castle with music. Cooks were preparing everything they could to make sure the feast was perfect, testing recipes and obtaining the best game and produce. New banners were hung along the stairs. A multitude of flower pots were gleaming, ready to be filled with flowers at the last minute. Garlands were ready to hang. The royal garden was groomed to perfection and even the center of the maze was made immaculate, though the King and Queen planned to keep it guarded to prevent anyone from wandering into it.

"That vixen is playing tricks on the Prince!" Even in his thoughts, he sounded indignant.

"He deserves the pranks," she shot back. *"And the pranks are*

clever but not harmful."

"Mayhaps so," he admitted. "What do you think of the Queen and King's plan?"

"Parents, even a King and Queen, can be sneaky," she thought.

"Especially if they truly love their child," he agreed.

"Still, the planning and preparations for a ball such as this, in just a month, is amazing!"

"They have a whole kingdom full of people they can command to help them. The King and Queen hardly have to do anything. Is it not the same today?"

"Today we hire someone called an event coordinator who handles the details."

Chapter Seven

Cinderella

Finally, it was the day before the grand ball. The town was swelling with people who came to attend the ball. Innkeepers were rubbing their hands in glee as noblemen and ladies of all descriptions came from every corner of the land, willing to pay any price for lodging. Commoners came flocking to the castle, even though accommodations were hard to find and vastly overpriced. Fathers and mothers were hoping their daughters would catch the Prince's eye. Tailors and seamstresses were nigh exhaustion from working all hours, day and night, sewing beautiful gowns and coats for people planning on attending the ball. Most of them had promised themselves that once their work was done, they would not even look at needle and thread for a month or more.

Even though she never got a gown for herself, and had no chance of going to the ball, Cinderella was kept extremely busy, especially that day, the day before the ball. She made last minute adjustments and fittings on the ball gowns for all three women. Since there had been no money to pay a seamstress, she had sewn the ball gowns for all three women herself, and it had been no easy task. They all wanted exquisite gowns with fancy beading and miles of lace, even feathers, with matching adornments for their hair.

Gertrude, who seemed oblivious to her age, had wanted a gown in brilliant blue, very tight at the waist and showing a daring décolletage. She was barely able to keep her breasts covered when she took a deep breath. Secretly, Cinderella enjoyed making that gown, knowing it made Gertrude look like a peacock, displaying her true age and exposing her as the low-class woman she truly was. It showed her vanity to perfection. Bridget, thin and petite, was by far the easiest to work with. She listened to Cinderella's suggestion for a pale yellow gown with moderate but effective trim, a décolletage that was low cut but not scandalous. The only problem Cinderella had with Bridget came when Bridget was driven almost to tears by her mother and Bianca. They each derided her gown, saying it was unflattering and far too plain. They also said the pale yellow satin was too common. Cinderella gently persuaded Bridget that the color of the gown set off her beauty, and made her complexion glow. She told her the style was indeed flattering, without being cheap and gaudy.

Bianca was the worst. Plump to the point of being fat, she wanted a red gown which made her complexion look sallow, and she insisted it be very form fitting and tight. She was harsh and demanding as she argued with Cinderella over every stitch. She was so crude and demanding Cinderella was astonished. She even threatened to beat Cinderella if her gown was not perfect. It was the final straw.

"Make your own gown, you selfish bitch!" she shouted at the shocked Bianca with a deadly insult. "I am not a servant here, I am a member of the family. I am my sire's true daughter, not some stepdaughter who was already an old maid when her mother married my father!"

"Old maid!" Bianca shrieked and slapped at Cinderella, who grabbed her hair and pulled it hard enough to remove a handful of the dull, limp brown hair.

The fight was on. Bianca swung wildly at Cinderella's face, and Cinderella dodged the slap easily, returning the blows with an ease that surprised even herself. It was a brief and violent battle that Cinderella won easily when she got a good shot at Bianca's ribs, robbing her of her breath. Cinderella worked hard every day, while Bianca sat around giving her orders and demanding service. Unfortunately, by the time Gertrude and Bridget got the two women separated, Bianca had a blackened eye, and her new gown was torn. Standing there, not even breathing heavily, Cinderella wondered vaguely where she had learned to fight so well.

Bianca cried for her mother to punish Cinderella but she was saved from any punishment by Gertrude simply because the older woman recognized Cinderella's fury and her strength. It was fear that stayed her hand. It was cowardice that made her begin to plot against Cinderella. She would get revenge. Cinderella might be strong but Gertrude was evil and devious.

Gertrude did not realize that Cinderella was devious too when pushed too hard, and Bianca had done it. She thought of a plan for quick revenge, and quietly put it into use. She made sure some of the seams in the gown were not properly sewn, and that they were ready to burst open.

As she helped the women get ready for the ball, she carefully helped Bianca into the gown, making sure she did not tear open the weakened seams. She also helped Gertrude and Bridget into their gowns. The two older women looked like vain peacocks, while Bridget looked sweet and charming.

Pretending meekness, Cinderella did the three women's hair in lavish styles, piled high atop their heads and threaded through with ribbons and lace to match their gowns.

She had the carriage as shiny and polished as she could make it, even the old mare was groomed until she shone. Cinderella had even managed to pay a local boy a few coins to drive the women to the ball.

They left for the ball early, excited and giggling. Gertrude was the worst of them because she seemed to believe that she could steal the Prince's heart. As usual, in her vanity, Gertrude forgot her age and acted like a schoolgirl. Bianca sat stiffly, her nose in the air, riding in a carriage that she felt was not up to her station. While Bridget did her best to look bored she was really excited. She had the strangest feeling that tonight she would find someone to love.

Cinderella was exhausted by the time she got the women dressed, coiffed, and into the carriage. In spite of the fact she was missing the ball, she enjoyed the peace and quiet of the empty cottage. Still, once the women were gone, she felt the hopelessness of being left behind and of not getting to see the Prince again crash over her. She still felt the need for revenge but admitted to herself that she had a growing interest in the Prince, almost an attraction, even though she was extremely angry with him.

As she realized she would not get to see the Prince she began to feel very sad, the comfort of the quiet cottage deserted her and waves of grief swept over her. She sat at the crude table and began to cry. There was a shadow of movement in the corner of the room. Cinderella looked over and saw a strange woman standing there with a gentle smile on her face.

"Who are you?" Cinderella jumped up, shocked. "What are you doing here?"

"Hello, my dear, I'm your fairy godmother," the old woman said with a gentle smile. "And I am here to make sure you get to the royal ball."

"I cannot go," Cinderella sighed sadly, sitting back down, slumping dejectedly in the wooden chair. "I have no carriage. I have no gown. I have no one to help me with my hair. I can't go even if I had those things because if Gertrude saw me there she would be so enraged, so angry, she would probably kill me."

"Now what kind of fairy godmother would I be if I could not handle those problems? That's nothing," the old woman said with a wide smile. "Trust me, Gertrude will be no problem, and you deserve to meet the Prince under better, more magical circumstances."

"Meet the Prince, again?" Cinderella said sharply. "I have met the Prince and I hate him. He spanked me over nothing! Why would I want to meet him again, especially when he's looking for a wife? All I want to do is take revenge on his royal self. I want to make damn sure he's paid well for spanking me."

"And what better way would there be to do that than to catch his eye and cause him to fall in love with you? Then drop him and break his heart, or even better yet, marry him and make his life miserable! Does that idea not hold some appeal?" The fairy godmother grinned at Cinderella's soft sly smile.

The fairy godmother conjured up a beautiful gown. It was soft pink satin, full and flowing with a daringly low neckline, showing off Cinderella's figure perfectly. It sparkled with jewels that were flattering but not excessive. She had Cinderella's hair elaborately styled atop her head, with a few tendrils curling down at the neck. Soon, out of nowhere, a beautiful coach appeared pulled by four dappled gray horses, all with beautiful conformation and long flowing manes and tails.

"Now before you get in the coach there something I must tell you, my dear, and this is very serious, mark my words well. If you stay at the ball too long the dress will revert back to your rags, and the coach and horses will disappear." She warned Cinderella, "You must be home by the last stroke of midnight."

"Thank you, fairy godmother." Cinderella hugged her. "This is going to be a wonderful night, I just know it. I do have one question maybe you can help me with. Do you know what happened to my father? And did Gertrude steal my father's fortune?"

"I cannae tell you all you want to know, my dear," she said sadly. "I can tell you Gertrude is evil and uses spells and potions to beguile men. I can also give you a clue where to look for the fortune. Your father hid his fortune in the house you grew up in, 'tis well hidden in the very same room you slept in. And I can tell you this, you will find justice for your father in the arms of the Prince. Now make haste, the Prince awaits!"

In spite of herself Cinderella arrived at the ball excited. There were so many grand sights and sounds, so many lovely ladies dressed in lavish gowns and courtly gentlemen in handsome coats and tight breeches, it was hard for her to remain aloof. Many people were dancing, swirling around the ballroom floor to a magnificent band, other people stood around the room and watched them. There were tables piled high with fine food and the wine was flowing freely.

Cinderella looked around at the sound of nervous laughter. A few of the guests were laughing at a woman, some were trying to be discreet, however others in the ballroom had no pretense at discretion. They laughed loudly and pointed. Cinderella knew instantly what was causing the uproar, still, she looked and saw Bianca in tears. The side of her gown, the seam that ran from beneath her arm to her waist, was slowly opening up. The area she had left weakened was indeed giving away, and soon, Bianca would have to leave the ball or face an even greater embarrassment. She felt no guilt or sympathy for her stepsister. Bianca had simply made her life a living torment for far too long.

On the other side of the room, Cinderella saw her stepsister Bridget talking earnestly with a man. He looked like he was in his mid-thirties, slightly balding, a little chubby and very ordinary. The one thing that stood out about him was that he seemed completely enamored with Bridget, and she seemed very happy talking to him. She seemed to almost glow under the attention of the man. Cinderella walked over to greet Bridget and meet this new man in her life.

"Cinderella! I am so pleased you managed to come to the ball," Bridget gushed. "Does Mother know you are here?"

"No," Cinderella said softly, "and I fear her reaction if she learns of it."

"Then I will not be the one who tells her. Cinderella, may I introduce you to Mr. Alesford?" Bridget smiled, a smile filled with more joy than Cinderella had ever seen on Bridget's face. "He's a fabric merchant from the south."

Cinderella greeted the man politely, then took Bridget aside. "It looks like you found your dream. I am very happy for you."

Susan Kohler

She hugged Bridget.

She walked away from Bridget, turned, and bumped into the Prince.

"May I have this dance?" he asked, giving a courtly bow before taking her arm and leading her to the dance floor.

He gave no sign he recognized her as they danced. In truth, he did not. His view of her from their previous meetings were mainly of her backside and her bare breasts. What he had seen of her face and clothes was a vision of dirt, crude cloth, and long black hair. He did not expect to see her here, in a beautiful gown, dressed and acting like a fine lady, who belonged in court attending royal balls.

She felt wonderful being held in his arms. They did not say a word but there was something magical about the night. Her heart was beating fast and hard as they moved slowly around the dance floor. He held her gently yet firmly, which made her feel cherished and protected as if she were precious to him. Without a word, as the music ended, he drew her out the side doors and into the fragrant garden. Their departure was noticed by the Queen, who nodded and whispered of it to the King when she saw the young couple walk through the door.

They strolled around the garden, talking quietly. Because of his duties, he couldn't spend too long with Cinderella or with any one woman, so he reluctantly led her back into the ballroom. She did not stay long in the ballroom however, she was restless and filled with new and turbulent emotions. She walked back out into the garden to take a moment by herself. As she sat quietly on a bench she heard three people talking. They were plotting against the Prince.

"Now you get him out here and cause an uproar. Tear your gown and scream," a male voice instructed. "I will come to your rescue and accuse him of molesting you. I will then force him to marry you for your honor."

"As if I had any." The woman had a brash laugh.

"By the time people come out here, you will have bruises on your face, and your hair will be torn down and tangled," he told her.

"You will make sure I have the bruises?" she asked him.

"Yea."

Cinderella peeked through the bushes and got a good look at the woman involved in the plot. She had some beauty, but there was a coarseness to her as well.

Before long, the Prince strolled out with that same woman on his arm. As the woman led him to a secluded spot, where she knew the two men were waiting, Cinderella stepped out of the bushes and slapped her across the face.

"Leave the Prince alone! I know your plot, you slut," Cinderella shouted.

The woman snarled at Cinderella before moving in to attack her. She grappled with the woman for a short time before the woman ran off crying. The Prince stared at Cinderella and finally, suddenly, recognized her. He was angry that she had been in a brawl with another woman and had run her off. He knew nothing of the plot against him, but he was stunned to find out the woman he thought was so beautiful and refined was the same one who had played the pranks on him.

"You! You look so different dressed like a lady instead of a slovenly slut. I thought I had found a woman I could care for and it turned out to be you, what a disappointment. I have had it with you!" The Prince dragged her over to the bench. "Why do you pester me all the time? Do you not dislike being spanked?" He sat down and began to pull her over his lap.

"No! You will not spank me again! I know not why I even tried, but I just saved you from a wench who was scheming to force you to marry her!" Cinderella ripped herself out of his grasp and ran, without realizing it, straight into the maze.

The Prince followed her. Neither of them was aware of the two guards, who happened to be the Prince's best guardsmen and also his friends, watching them with amusement. Neither of them was aware that the guards let them pass, and for certain neither of them was aware of the legend attached to the maze. Cinderella ran blindly, turning right and left, only intent on escaping him. She could hear him running behind her. After several turns, she found herself in the center of the maze. There was a white gazebo surrounded by magnificent flowers that scented the evening air. There was also a beautiful fountain just at the entrance to the gazebo, filling it with the sound of flowing water. Inside the gazebo there was a plush chaise lounge covered in red velvet. It was there the Prince caught up with her.

Suddenly, in the fragrant garden, lit by torches, he saw her in a whole new light. He was instantly aroused, he had to have her. She looked at him as a chill of arousal ran down her spine and all thoughts of fleeing from him, and even all thoughts of revenge left her mind, leaving only desire. She knew nothing of love. Her only knowledge of mating came from watching her mare and the Prince's stallion. She also knew nothing of sex. She only knew she wanted this man to put his hands on her, and that she wanted something more. They came together, kissing and holding each other. Without a word, he began to remove her clothes, at first gently, then with growing desperation. She made no objection, indeed, without a word, she turned, giving him access to the laces running down her back. Not even knowing why or how she knew what would please him, she turned back, smiling and began to unfasten his breeches.

Finally, he spoke, "I know not your name, nor anything about you but I need you as much as I need my next breath."

"As I need you, Milord. I have never felt like this." Cinderella sighed, then had a sudden flash of panic. "I am afraid though. Are we truly alone here? What if somebody comes? I am unclothed!"

"My sire set guards around the maze to keep people out." He kissed her and she forgot her fears. "I thank the Lord he picked two who are friends as well as guards to me, else you would have never been allowed to enter the maze."

With that, the time for talking ended. They melted onto the soft cushions of the chaise and began kissing each other. His hands stroked gently over her body, his mouth feasted on her neck. She moaned and her head fell back to give him better access to her throat. Slowly his mouth followed his hands as they trailed down her body and she began to quiver as those magic hands and that daring mouth aroused her.

She writhed under him. She began to use her hands and mouth as he used his on her. It seemed to inflame him even further. She stroked delicate fingers over the nipples on his chest, following her hands with her mouth, teasing and tasting him. He continued his own travels down her body, caressing her breasts and sucking her nipples before letting his mouth travel down to explore her ribs, her navel, her soft flat stomach, and trail even lower to take her in an intimate kiss. She screamed her pleasure, squirming in painful ecstasy.

He rose up to take her mouth as he entered her. He was not surprised to find the entrance blocked by her hymen, and with one fierce pushed he broke through the barrier. Then he held himself still, with a great effort, letting her settle and go past the pain to the pleasure. She had indeed felt the pain, but it was overwhelmed by the sensations she felt and the sense of power it gave her to have the Prince quivering atop her. In a few brief seconds, he began to move inside her, building up the speed and power of his thrusts. He rode her hard and fast and she met him thrust for thrust until they collapsed together in an orgasmic heap.

They lay like that for a long moment tangled and sated. Finally, they realized they should get up and dress. She stood up and he helped her with her gown but nothing could help her hair, it had come down and was flowing around her shoulders. Just as they kissed, she heard the clock began to strike midnight.

Panicked, she broke away from him and ran, losing a shoe as she hurried away. Since he still had no clothes on, she was too fast for him to catch. So he dressed and returned to the ball.

His mother and father knew he'd been with a woman the minute he entered the ballroom. They looked at each other with love and amusement, both hoping that he had not made love in the center of the maze. They both knew how powerful the legend was. There was nothing to do for it, but to enjoy the rest of the ball and talk about it tomorrow.

Cinderella ran but she was not fast enough to get home before her gown turned back to rags and the carriage disappeared. She wound up walking until her feet were aching and blistered, almost bleeding. Her stepmother, along with Bianca and Bridget, were already home. Bianca could be heard crying from her room.

Bridget was excited about her new male friend, but she was keeping her excitement to herself. She was smart enough to know that her mother and sister would resent her for finding someone and would do their best to ruin her happiness. For the first time, she truly knew how Cinderella felt and began to regret her part in how she had treated her.

"Where have you been, you worthless chit?" Gertrude called out furiously as Cinderella entered the cottage. "We need your help getting out of these gowns."

"'Tis no business of yours where I've been or what I've been doing. Undress yourselves!" Cinderella shouted back, her hands defiantly planted on her hips.

"You worthless slut! You will do as I say!" Gertrude seemed almost dangerously insane as she shouted at Cinderella.

Cinderella did not know how upset and truly angry Gertrude was. Gertrude had used her potion to blind the Prince to her true age and nature. She did not know Cinderella had weakened the potion when she emptied out most of the contents of the vial and replaced it with dirty water. All she knew was the potion had not worked. In truth, the Prince was curt and dismissive when talking with her. It was plain he could not be less interested in anything about her.

Cinderella, perhaps unwisely, snarled at Gertrude, "Leave off, you evil witch, I will not do your bidding."

Ignoring the sudden flush of anger on Gertrude's face, she stomped off towards her pallet and threw herself on it to remember how it felt to make love to the Prince. She needed to try to sleep because she knew there would be chores to do in the morning. And she wanted to find a way to be with the Prince again.

"A fairy godmother? Seriously?" Cyn laughed softly.

"She did well for Cinderella. She got her to the ball in a gorgeous dress. Now it's up to Cinderella to catch the Prince's eye."

"She will, I trust her to be able to entice the Prince." Cyn was determined.

"Since she looks like you, in fact, is you, I am sure she can do it. From what I have seen, you can entice almost any man, especially swimming in a pond without any clothes." She felt his laugh.

"Well, truth be told, you look pretty terrific swimming nude as well. You also look great in your formal clothes." She batted her eyelashes at him in an exaggerated and flirtatious manner.

"Thank you, Milady." He thought, "Look, they are entering the maze!"

"Now we will learn about the lege… oh my goodness!" She saw clothing being removed.

"Yes, it looks good to me." They watched the couple, themselves, make love.

"Men, in any century, are predictable, it seems, thank heaven." She drawled.

"And women are always unpredictable, thank heaven." He laughed.

She felt his smile and thought, "I pray we get to make love, really make love and not just in a dream."

"I do as well, lass. I do as well." He agreed.

Suddenly she felt an awareness, a sense of danger. *"We must see what's happening in my room. I feel danger!"*

Together they looked in on her body. She had healed some and looked a little better but she was still unconscious. Bridget and Bianca were there, looking at her with sadness and some sympathy. It was Gertrude though who surprised her. Gertrude visiting her in the hospital? Something was very wrong.

As soon as she had the thought she heard Gertrude say, *"Well, what do you mean she's not brain dead? She's obviously not in there. I know she's an organ donor so declare her brain dead and harvest her organs! It's what she'd want!"*

"What is she trying to do?" Robbie was puzzled.

"If I were declared brain dead, they could take my heart and some other parts to give to someone who needs them to live. I believe in that but only if I'm brain dead, beyond any hope. She doesn't care about helping others, she just wants me dead."

The doctor standing by her bed looked at Gertrude in disgust. *"First of all, Ma'am, she is not brain dead, there are some indications of life, not many but some. Also, I am not her primary physician, I will consult with him in the morning. I do know you haven't been visiting or even asking about her in all the time she's been here. I also know she is very rich. I suspect you are after her money and care nothing for her."*

Gertrude snarled at the doctor, turned and left the room in ICU. Even in her state, (was it limbo?), Cyn was shaking and irate. *"That bitch is trying to kill me!"*

"Yea, lass, that she is."

Soon Cyn had another visitor. She hadn't known but one of the policemen who had been at the scene of her accident was investigating the case. He had suspicions. He spoke to the doctor who had seen Gertrude that evening.

The young resident gave him an earful. *"It was weird like she wanted Cyn declared brain dead,"* he told the detective. *"Most relatives fight against it, but not her. She wanted Cynthia declared brain dead and her organs harvested."*

"Gertrude Snowden is an interesting woman," the detective said cautiously. "I shouldn't be telling you this but everything she has, she inherited. Several husbands have made her a wealthy widow. I fear for Cynthia because she inherited millions from her father, and I know Mrs. Snowden wants it."

"What can we do?" the doctor asked.

"I will work on a restraining order to keep her away from Cynthia. I have enough to lay it out to a judge. Meanwhile, you can tell everyone up to the hospital administration that she is not to be alone with Cynthia, not for a second."

"We will protect her," the doctor said with conviction.

"I'm working on getting the evidence I need to put this monster away for life." The detective shook hands with the doctor and left.

Chapter Eight

Cinderella

At the palace the next morning, when the Prince first woke up, he sought out his mother and father. He found them in the great dining hall, breaking their fast.

"Honored Sire and my Lady mother, I must tell you I fell in love last night, truly in love. I have found the woman I wish to marry, with your permission." His speech was formal, but his smile was wide and warm.

"Who is this woman who has captured your heart, my son?" the King asked.

"I do not know her name," the Prince admitted. "She left in a hurry after we made lo-."

He stopped talking as the Queen gasped. "Where, my son? Where did you bed this woman?"

"'Twas in the center of the maze." He smiled at the memory.

"And you know not her name or her station?" the King questioned.

"No, Sire," he said slowly.

"How will you find her again my son?" the Queen asked gently.

"All I have of her is a shoe, and a vague idea of where she lives," the Prince admitted ruefully. "I know that she is beautiful, and she was a virgin. And I know that I love her with all my heart, and she would make a wonderful wife for me and a very suitable mother for my children."

"Then we shall find her, my son," the King said. "But first, we have to ask you, have you ever heard of a legend about the maze."

"Nay, Sire." The Prince was interested. "What is the legend?"

"The legend is that if a couple finds each other in the center of the maze, without a map or any other guide or aid, and makes love there, they are fated to be together forever." The Queen smiled softly at a memory. "It ran true for your father and myself. You were born less than a year after our first time in the maze."

"Then we must find the lass." The Prince was adamant. "As soon as we can."

Men were sent out with decrees to find the lass.

Cinderella woke that morning in a great mood. She snuggled briefly on her pallet, reveling in her memories of the night before. Her peace and quiet were soon shattered as her two stepsisters were both ill. Shortly after their morning meal, they both began feeling queasy and vomited. It seemed they had overindulged at the ball, feasting on the lavish food and drinking too much wine. Cinderella tended to them as best as she could, delaying her chance to find a way to go to the Prince at the castle.

When Gertrude learned of the men searching for Cinderella she was enraged. She wanted the Prince for herself and she was furious that somehow Cinderella had made it to the ball and captured the heart of the Prince. She came up with a plan to discredit her and make it impossible for Cinderella and the Prince to wed. She dressed herself in one of her most discreet gowns and went to the castle.

"I have to tell you something, Your Highness," she said to the King. "I regret to tell you that I have a stepdaughter who is a slut with low morals and a thieving nature. I fear she has made advances on your son."

Gertrude went on to tell the King all the lies she could think of, making Cinderella sound as terrible as she possibly could. She mentioned Cinderella spent a lot of time drinking and wasting time at a local tavern known to be frequented by the lowest scum. According to Gertrude, Cinderella was adept at picking up men and blinding them with her beauty. She said that Cinderella would steal from them when she bedded them down. And that she would have sex with strange men for money. According to Gertrude, she was a prostitute, a slut, and a thief. In fact, Gertrude hinted that Cinderella may have killed her own father for his fortune, and let it drop that her own two daughters were violently ill, mayhaps poisoned. She was very believable, offering to bring witnesses to the girl's bad behavior, and soon the King and Queen were very worried about their son.

The King sent for his son, and the Prince arrived shortly. "My son, it has come to my attention that the woman you claim to love is a very low character, totally unsuited to marry into the royal family. She has no family name and is only called slut by those who speak of her. I learned this when a woman came to warn me about her. She has been telling us about the woman you claim to love and she has said enough for me to have the woman brought in for questioning. She has even offered to bring in witnesses, and she has shown me some proof. I am sorry, my son, but I am sending my men to bring her in and if they do not find her I will post a reward. If what I have heard is true, she should be imprisoned instead of marrying a prince."

"'Tis all lies, I would swear to it, I tell you!" The Prince stalked around the room in agitation. "I know she is an innocent."

The King was unmoved, he was far too worried for his son to be appeased. Neither the King nor the Queen would listen as the Prince tried to defend his love. They felt he was blinded by the lust and attraction he felt for the strumpet. The Prince left in a fit of temper, riding out on his black stallion in such a rush to get to his lady that he left his guards behind.

The guards stood up for the Prince and explained what they knew about Cinderella, including her real name. It seemed her father was a nobleman and had been a great friend to the King. The King felt bad because he had lost track of the man's daughter when her father died unexpectedly. The guards had done some investigating and learned quite a bit about Gertrude and about the death of Cinderella's father. They described how hard Cinderella worked and how she was treated by her stepmother, as if she were the lowest servant instead of the beloved daughter of a nobleman, and how Gertrude lost or spent her husband's fortune leaving Cinderella impoverished.

When the Queen left the room for a moment, the two guards gave the King a humorous and slightly risqué tale of how the Prince and Cinderella had first met. They talked about her pranks, stealing his clothes and putting a snake in his boot. The King was laughing as the Queen came back into the room. They also reminded the King and Queen that Cinderella had found the center of the maze without help. They knew the legend about that maze. It was said that whoever found the center without help would marry the next heir to the throne. And there was something magical about making love in the maze, it seems to lead to pregnancy.

The Queen turned to the King with a wide smile. "Remember at the start of summer when we went into the maze? We need to find out the truth, our son loves this girl."

Bridget found out what Gertrude was doing and decided to help Cinderella. For once in her life, she took a stand against her evil mother and warned Cinderella that her mother would swear out a complaint against her with the King. Gertrude was not above bribing men to besmirch Cinderella's name. Evidence could be forged.

Bridget had sent word to Mr. Alesford to come help her. The man had a great idea for hiding Cinderella. It seemed that as a fabric merchant he sold fabric to a traveling acting troupe. He got one of the actors to come with him and help him disguise Cinderella. By the time they finished with Cinderella, it was almost impossible to recognize her. She looked heavier with the aid of some padding. She had a wig that made her hair look stringy and gray, and she walked with a cane. Make-up to give her wrinkles completed the disguise.

Then Mr. Alesford took Cinderella up into the hills to stay with a friend and his family. Cinderella was almost happy taking care of the family's seven small boys, but still, she wanted to get word to the Prince and restore her good name.

The King was no fool. He had been shocked and angry listening to Gertrude, but as he calmed down and thought about it, he mistrusted the woman. He had three reasons for his mistrust. First, the woman tried far too hard to convince him the lass was evil. He was canny enough to know that evil could hide behind a pretty face but he remembered the young woman he had seen dancing with the Prince and found it nigh impossible to see true evil in her. Her accuser, however, seemed not only capable of true evil but he sensed a hint of insanity in her.

Then, he trusted his son's judgment. The Prince still had traces of his boyhood in him, but the King could see the man he soon would be. He was maturing daily, gaining insight into people and learning to read situations. There was nothing that could blind him to that degree to the evil residing in a woman. Finally, there was the legend of the maze. The King knew from personal experience the legend held true. It had for his own parents, and for him and his Queen. He believed it held true for the Prince as well.

He called in some advisers who had known her father. He consulted them on the character of the late nobleman and of his family. To a man, they were suspicious of his death. None of them knew what had happened to his fortune or to his young child, his daughter. The man had kept her away from most of them but those who knew her called her a delightful child, on the verge of young womanhood. All the men expressed a deep mistrust or even outright hatred of his last wife. Some even had outright suspicions about his death.

"Why have none of you spoken to me of your suspicions?" the King demanded with a trace of anger.

"Your Highness, none of us had any proof," one of the men told him.

The King sent the men from the room. He sat and thought. The Queen came in, excited, and interrupted his thoughts. "My husband," she told him, "I think I am with child."

The news stopped his pondering for a time as he hugged his wife. Then he told her all of his thoughts and all he had learned.

"You must act as if you believed Gertrude," the Queen said wisely. "Else you put Cinderella in even greater danger from the woman. She must be quite mad."

"I agree, wife," the King gave his wife a look of warmth and desire. "I will say naught of this, except to warn the men I have searching for the girl to make sure they bring her to me without harm. Woe to the man who injures her in any way."

He called his men in and gave that order. He stood watching as they left to obey him before he turned to his lady wife.

"And now, my love, let us retire to our chamber and celebrate the coming child."

The Queen smiled widely. "With pleasure, Milord, with pleasure."

The Prince rode all over the countryside trying to find Cinderella. He looked for her everywhere but he could not find her. She knew she was being hunted by the King's men but not why. She thought Gertrude was behind it and that she was in danger if found. The Prince had no idea that she had left the family she had been staying with. Now she was constantly moving, avoiding detection by going from place to place, usually stopping in spots that had already been searched. She kept her disguise at all times.

He could not find her anywhere until he circled back on his search. He rode up into the hills far from the crude hut where he had first seen Cinderella. One day he stopped in a small village and saw an old crone. She didn't look anything like Cinderella but there was something in the way she moved that seemed strangely youthful, and something in the way she looked at him that made him wonder. He reached into his cloak pocket and pulled out the shoe he had put there after the ball. He had carried it with him everywhere, as a talisman. He approached the old crone, asking her to sit on a stool and to try on the shoe to see if it fit. As he gently lifted her foot he looked into her eyes and knew, so he began to gently slide the shoe onto...

Robbie and Cyn left as soon as the Prince slid the shoe onto Cinderella's foot. They found themselves in a stone castle.

In the hospital, Cyn's doctor stood and looked at the patient he'd been treating for such a long time. Outwardly, most of her injuries had healed, there was little scarring left, thanks to a great plastic surgeon.

Although it was unprofessional, he was drawn to this patient, almost in love with her. It was something he never told any of the other staff, fearing they'd either laugh at him or report him to the hospital administration. He knew hope was fading but there was still a kernel of hope.

As he had done often before, he tested for a reaction from her. It was an old test, not one of the newer methods, but it was quick and not invasive. He gently lifted her foot, cupping the heel. He stroked a finger along the sole. He'd done it before, many times, with no sign of a reaction. This time he got one. Her toes curled, a tiny motion, but a motion.

He waited a few moments and tried it again to see if it was truly a reaction or just a fluke. She reacted once again, curling her toes as if ticklish. She did not wake up but for the first time, he felt real hope. He fought the urge, the highly improper urge, to kiss her. Instead, he said a silent prayer of thanks and for her continued healing before he went on with his rounds.

Chapter Nine

Snow White

Cynthia woke up confused and disoriented, in a room totally unfamiliar to her. She remembered her apartment in New York and her horse ranch in Tennessee. She knew who she was, she was Cynthia Wright Snowden. She felt the overwhelming grief of her father's sudden, shocking death. She remembered her stepmother Gertrude, and her two stepsisters, Bianca and Bridget. She knew they wanted to take control of the ranch, the apartment, her brothers, and everything she had inherited from her wealthy father. She had met with her lawyer to block Gertrude, and on the way home from the meeting something happened. She saw a bus bearing down on her and... She heard a strange beeping sound as she drifted back to sleep.

She woke again. This time she seemed to be in a crude cottage. There were no modern conveniences. She ached from head to toe from doing constant chores. Her brothers were not around. She instinctively knew her father was dead. He would never leave her in such a hovel doing all the tasks. She heard her stepmother's strident voice calling her.

"Cinderella! Get in here and fix our breakfast!"

She decided Cinderella was a wimp who did not stand up for herself. It was her last thought as she drifted, once again, off to sleep.

This time when she woke she was snuggled in a comfortable bed. There was a soft feather mattress, clean white linens, and a warm woolen blanket on the bed. As she looked around, her eyes still only half-open, she noted that the large bedchamber had stone walls and looked like it should have been cold, but instead it was warm with a fire blazing in a small fireplace in the corner. Near the fireplace there was a small sturdy table, its dark wood intricately carved, and a comfortable wooden chair. A thick woven rug covered the stone floor. An elaborately carved wooden wardrobe stood along one wall. There was a copper bathtub sitting in front of the small fire, filled with steamy water.

Cynthia sat up in the bed and puzzled over this. Where was she? This was certainly not the modern home she remembered, nor was it the crude hut she hated. Her vague memories were only of the two very different places. The first was the crowded city that seemed to be filled with wonders she could not begin to understand, and even as she had those memories they began to grow vague and dim. Noises and smells, strange conveyances, and smooth paths filled with people started to fade.

The other place rapidly fading from her memory was the crude hut. She remembered endless chores, as well as her stepmother and two stepsisters ordering her about constantly. Her two stepsisters were almost as bad as her stepmother. Neither of them did any chores. All of the onerous tasks fell to her. She knew she cared for the animals, planted the small garden, and cooked and cleaned in the small hovel. She had scenes of laundry, sewing, and emptying chamber pots in her head. They faded even as she began to wonder where she was now and why she wasn't back in the crude hut. Once more she drifted off to sleep.

When she woke once again she was in a place where there were no modern conveniences. Once again she was stuck with only a chamber pot. When, she wondered, would she find herself in a place where there were things like telephones, central heating, and even a working toilet? Even as she thought these things, her memories of them faded until they seemed only a crazy myth. What exactly was a working toilet? She shook her head in curiosity, deciding to get up and dressed before she went out in search of some very important answers.

She left the bed and dropped her nightgown to the floor. She walked over to the tub, noting the rose petals and other flowers floating on the water. How had they known when she would awaken, she wondered, and how had they managed to fill the tub without waking her?

She put those questions aside and sank into the hot water. She reveled in the bath, scrubbing herself clean with soap that seemed crude but was scented with flowers. With a sigh, she decided it was time to get out.

Just as she rose from the tub and reached for a towel there was a knock on the door.

"Snow, dear," the voice had her stepsister Bridget's familiar high-pitched whine, "you had best hurry with your bath and get dressed. Quickly now! Father has a special guest coming today and he is quite insistent that we all meet him." Her voice dropped to a loud whisper. "You will never guess who he is."

"I give up, who is he?" Cynthia asked with little interest in the mystery guest.

Her heart was racing from the news that her beloved father was alive, and apparently well, in this strange reality. In her dreams, he was dead! She realized she was in an ancient era. Was it medieval, she wondered? She used the chamber pot with disgust.

As Bridget spoke, the name she had called her, Snow, began to register. Snow White? She barely remembered being Cynthia, but the name acted as a trigger and she forgot Cynthia as she began to understand more and more of the pieces of Snow White's life.

"His name is Prince Robert, and he is rumored to be young, single, rich, and very handsome." Bridget sighed in delight as she continued to talk softly to Cynthia through the door. "He is even richer than Father, I mean, his kingdom is. I think Father wants to match him to one of us. He would make a terrific husband."

Cynthia quickly pulled on a robe and opened the door. She

saw Bridget standing there dressed in a very fancy dress with lace at the bodice and covered in tiny pearls. She looked wonderful and Cynthia told her so.

"Thank you, Snow." Bridget came in and sat on Snow's bed. She was slender and not a true beauty, but she was pretty, especially when she was happy and smiling. She wore a pale pink gown that suited her coloring and made her slender curves look enticing.

"It will probably be Bianca he is matched with since she is the eldest," Snow said, warning both herself and Bridget not to get their hopes up.

"I know," Bridget admitted.

"Nevertheless, I'll be right out, Bridget," Snow said as she turned to the wardrobe, "as soon as I finish dressing." She rang for her maid.

She did indeed hurry. Not from any eagerness to see her father's guest, but from eagerness to see her father. She dressed in the rather childish clothes she found in the wardrobe.

"Bridget," she asked her stepsister, "where are my nice clothes? There are only a few skirts and blouses in here. I know I should have some rich gowns such as yours. Why do I only have childish clothes?"

Bridget could not hide her nervousness as she fumbled for an answer. "Snow, you are so much younger than I am, even more so than Bianca. Surely that is the reason for your childish clothes. You are still a child."

"Bah!" Snow snorted. "I am no child. In many instances I would be considered an old maid," her eyes narrowed before continuing, "as would you."

Bridget sniffed at the insult, her eyes filling with tears as she left the room without a word. Snow's maid, who had the sense to wait until Bridget left, came into the room. Snow turned back to the wardrobe and looked once again at the contents. There was a clean white blouse with lace on the sleeves, a bright blue skirt, a soft blue over-skirt, and white stockings with blue shoes.

"Where are your fine clothes, Milady?" her maid asked, aghast at what she saw in the wardrobe.

"I know not," Snow said softly, "but I need to dress and go to Father, quickly. I will have to wear these."

With the maid fussing over her, Snow did indeed dress quickly. She put on the blue skirt and white blouse. Around her waist, she put a wide black belt. Her maid brushed her hair and pulled it back into a blue mesh snood. Snow quickly checked the mirror. Deciding she looked presentable, although assuredly juvenile, she left the room and went in search of her father.

She found herself atop a long curved staircase made of stone. The staircase opened to the great room of a rich castle. There were torches on the walls, giving off a soft light. She could see rich tapestries and several oil paintings. The tapestries were mainly hunting scenes, with a couple devoted to biblical scenes, and the paintings seemed to be mainly family portraits. Along the front of the room there was a raised area where her father could sit with his wife and daughters and watch the room. In front of the raised area running across the room was a long, carved, wooden table with cushioned chairs. There were other long tables running perpendicular to this table, not as elaborate, and with benches instead of chairs.

The whole room looked rich for this time. Apparently here her father was a nobleman, perhaps even the King himself. She had few memories of this life, but of another life, another time. Those memories were rich indeed. She had memories of growing up with a father's love and a wonderful mother who died far too young. She also had memories of a vain, resentful stepmother, and two pampered, thoughtless stepsisters.

Her stepmother had treated her kindly in public but privately she was entirely different. Snow had always mistrusted her. She got along well enough with the two stepsisters, but without any real warmth between them. The two women were much too jealous of Snow's looks and friendly manner for them to be as close as Snow would have liked.

Also, in that half-remembered life, she knew that her father had married often, but not well, and he had given her seven small half- and stepbrothers. The boys kept her hopping, but she really loved the band of scamps. Where were they in this world? It seems her life was generally full of peace and joy. The vague memories of another life, already fading, were troubling. She remembered being happy until the sudden and mysterious death of her father had shocked her, and turned her very existence upside down.

Snow shook her head at the memories; they were false, a trick of some kind, since her father was indeed alive. Even as she had the awful memories, they began to fade and leave her with nothing but a firm distrust of Gertrude and her two daughters. Other memories danced just under the horizon of her awareness, teasing her with glimpses of a different life. Once again she had a fleeting glimpse of a crude hut filled with anger and endless chores.

Snow found her father downstairs in the library. He was dressed as richly as if he were, indeed, the King. At the sight of him, she was filled with a moment of full awareness. The memories of this life sprang into bloom, and she knew who she was and what her life was like in this reality.

At that moment she became Snow, truly Snow, and all her other memories faded away completely. She knew, at that moment, that her father was truly the King. She knew they lived in a castle high on a hill overlooking his kingdom. It was not a very large or important kingdom but the land was fertile, the kingdom was prosperous and the people were happy. The King loved his life and his kingdom. Although he had lived a reckless, even sinful life, the King had matured. Now, in most ways, he was a pious and temperate man with an even nature.

He drank little, ate well and was still fit and trim. He gambled only moderately. He kept his army well prepared but used his skill at negotiation to avoid war when possible. He and his family lived comfortably but not extravagantly. He had a small chapel built on one side of the castle, and the priest was a kindly, cheerful man of the Lord. Both the King and Snow tried to follow the Lord's way and visited the chapel daily. Gertrude and both girls avoided the place as if entering the chapel would bring on eternal damnation.

Still, the King had one real vice: women. The King loved women. It was not the courting of women he loved, nor just being around them. No, he loved bedding women.

Although he had repented, he had his memories of them. Ladies, wenches, serfs, or sluts, he had cared naught which they were. Nor had he cared if they were young or old, thin or heavy, comely or plain. As long as they had a certain joy in their heart, some zest for life, and were willing to spend a few pleasant hours with him, he had bedded them. His one saving grace was that he was kind to the women he bedded and took care of his offspring, legitimate or not.

Not that all women were the same to him, really. He was a man who had known well the full depths and heights true love can reach. His first bride, the wife of his heart, had died of a fever when their daughter, Snow, their only child, was but four years old. A series of dalliances with local women had left him, it was said, with as many as seven small sons. Some were his actual sons and some were stepsons. The King cared for them all. Just who and where they were was a mystery. Some wondered if the boys really even existed. Snow was the only one who knew the truth. She privately thought it was well that they were hidden away to protect them from Gertrude.

There was another woman who was different from the rest, his latest, Gertrude. Since his marriage to Gertrude he had forgone even his love of bedding women, although there was no love between him and his wife. It was not merely that he did not love her, in truth, he hated her with a passion that startled even him with its intensity. He often wondered why he had wed the lady but even with the perfect wisdom of hindsight he still found no answer.

Oh, there were many reasons he could name: financial and political gain, her prominent family name and social connections, but these turned out to be illusions. She had no money, no social status, no familial connections. She was a fraud. That galled a king who was known for keen judgment and insight. He had also wanted a second mother for Snow, and he thought she would grow to love his daughter as she loved her own girls.

The girls, both several years older than Snow, were also both disappointments because they were jealous of Snow's grace and beauty. Still, the girls were not vicious, just thoughtless, and he had hopes for them. His last reason for marrying Gertrude was that he had wanted still more sons, legitimate sons. He also wanted a companion to rule by his side.

These reasons were almost enough for the marriage, but there was something more, there had to be. By some means, she had deceived him as to her real character. He had loved and bedded many women over the years but he had never before been blinded by a woman's true nature. Now, he secretly feared that he had not yet seen the depths to which she could sink.

The King had also loved another woman, a very young woman, his beautiful daughter the Royal Princess Snow. In spite of her unusual name and her title, she was a sweet-natured, innocent lass with a soft ready smile, genuine warmth, and was caring in her manner towards all people. He had trained her to rule since she was born and knew her nature: a combination of gentleness and strength, tempered with sound judgment, would serve her well.

She was not some gentle flower who sat in the salon and sewed or read poetry. Indeed, Princess Snow was adept with bow and arrows, but she seldom hunted herself. She would ride out with him because she loved to ride, but she preferred target shooting over killing live game. Snow was also skilled with a sword, having pestered some of her father's guards into giving her lessons much to her father's secret pride and feigned dismay. She was also extremely good with all animals, especially her horses. She was the joy of her father's life and he was the heart of her world.

Snow paused, looking at her father. She still had vague memories, strange ones, of a former life, but they seemed just strange dreams. To her, this was reality and she realized that in this reality she was Snow White. She knew it was a tale, but she could not remember how the tale progressed or how it ended. The words 'happily ever after' floated through her mind. She smiled to herself, good enough, she thought.

She quickly walked over to her father and hugged him with all the love she had never again thought she'd be able to show him.

"Good morning, Father." She kissed his cheek. "How are you today?"

"I'm fine, Daughter." Her father hugged her in return. "You seem to be very full of life's joy today."

"'Tis just that I am so happy to see you." Snow studied her father's face.

He had a handsome face, barely lined with age, tan skin and deep blue eyes. He had a dimple in his chin and winning smile. His hair was silver gray and cut short, but not exceedingly short. He was well built but not really slender, the years had filled out his frame just enough to give him added stature. He was a kind, intelligent man, with a warm heart and real joy and affection for his family, except for his wife.

"Daughter, you act like you haven't seen me in ages, yet 'twas only yesterday since we talked," he said with some amusement.

"I know, Father, but sometimes I feel that I fail to tell you often enough how much I cherish you and how lucky I am to have you for a father." Snow hugged him again. "If I do, I will never forgive myself."

"And I love you, Snow, my dear." He smiled down at her. "Truly I am the lucky one, to have a daughter such as you."

As the moment passed, Snow looked up at her father and asked, "So who's this guest you've invited to share our home for a few days? Bridget said he's royal, rich and handsome. Of course, Bridget thinks almost any man is handsome."

"Prince Robert?" her father asked with a twinkle in his eye. "He's just passing through. He seems to be most worthy though, and he is certainly royal and rich. Handsome? I cannot say, I do not look for that in a man. He's a fine young man though. His father, who is the King from the other side of the mountains, is a very dear old friend of mine so I thought I would let his son meet my three beautiful daughters. 'Tis sad but true that soon I must search out husbands for the three of you. I had Bianca take him for a walk in the garden."

"Do you think he will marry her?" Snow asked without real interest.

"Bianca?" Her father thought for a moment. "Nay, lass, she's a bit too old for the likes of him." He looked at Snow with studied casualness. "Why are you dressed in such childish clothes? Surely, there are more suitable gowns in your wardrobe."

"Truly, Sire, this was all I could find," Snow told him softly.

"I know you have many beautiful gowns, gowns that make you look breathtaking. I wonder then, who is jealous of your beauty," he mused. "Couldst mayhaps be either of your two stepsisters or could even be my wife."

"Gertrude?" Snow was astonished. "Why would she do such a thing?"

"She is a vain woman and exceedingly jealous of your youth and beauty. Also, she knows you are my one true heir, so you stand to inherit the kingdom. And lastly, she knows you will probably make the most advantageous marriage due to your fortune, status, and beauty, not to mention that you have a very pleasing nature."

"I hate this talk of inheriting, Sire." She felt a shiver of warning run down her spine. "I do not want to inherit anything from you, I want to have you here with me, in my life, for a long, long time."

"And you shall, my dear child, you shall." He kissed her cheek. "Still, Snow, my daughter, I must talk to you about Gertrude. I have passed a decree that makes her my consort but not my queen. If anything ever happens to me, you shall reign."

"Father! Naught will happen to you," Snow protested.

"I hope not, Snow, but I must plan for any happening." The King sighed. "Gertrude is an evil woman. She kept her true nature hidden from me until we were wed, but she is wicked. Never trust her."

"Then send her away from here," Snow protested. "Divorce her!"

"I cannot," the King said sadly, "and I must protect her daughters. I fear for them, as they do not know the full range of her wickedness."

"Surely she would not harm her own daughters!" Snow was shocked.

"I hope not, as they are innocent of her evildoing," the King said, "but they are not overly bright. They are thoughtless and jealous of you. Neither of them has your beauty nor your brains, and they certainly do not have Gertrude's talent for bewitching a man. They do have good hearts. Help them if you can."

"Yes, Father," Snow said firmly as she began to pace around the room, "but you will be here to help them."

"Of course I will," he paused and reached out to take her hand, "but if I'm not, Snow, find the boys, my boys, and protect them." He looked at her earnestly.

"The boys?" Snow asked. "Your sons?"

"My bastards some call them," the King said softly. "You must have heard the rumors, the talk about the seven of them.

You are the only one who knows the truth of it. You know where I have them secreted in the woods, away from Gertrude and her mischief. You know of the caretaker I have hired to raise them, their teacher, and the guards to protect them. I fear she would harm them thinking I want a male heir. I want them raised well and protected, but you are to be my heir. The daughter of my one true Queen."

"Then why hide the boys away, Father?" Snow asked.

"Because Gertrude is the kind of woman who would see my sons, even my illegitimate sons, as a larger threat to the throne than my daughter, whatever my wishes in the matter," he told her.

"But, Sire, if aught were to happen to you, Lord forbid, Gertrude would hide any decree you left, or burn it and deny it ever existed," Snow pointed out, "and declare herself Queen."

"The Royal Decree I made has been copied and sent-" The King stopped speaking as he heard Gertrude's voice sounding very near.

He wanted to tell Snow that his decree had been sent to the next kingdom for safekeeping and to tell her that she could trust that king. He decided to wait until Gertrude was not around. He was still a healthy man, surely he had time left to make such preparations.

He merely said, "These plans will never be necessary. Nothing will happen to me. Gertrude dares not harm me."

"Of course not, Father." She adored her father. They both put the unpleasant discussion out of their minds and talked of more pleasant things.

"So that is your father, lass. He seems kind and loving," Robbie muttered.

"Yes, it's good to see him again. He was a very good man, kind and funny and fair. I loved him very much. He died last winter, in my real life." Her grief was so palpable even Robbie, who had never met her father, could feel it.

"How did he die? He seemed in the best of health, hale and hearty." Robbie wondered.

"He was. He died suddenly and mysteriously. The autopsy said it was possibly poison. I suspect Gertrude had him killed." Her tone was bitter.

"What is an autopsy?"

"A specially trained doctor examines the body, even the internal organs, to determine the cause of death. They do it to learn more about how to save lives and to decide if a death should be investigated as a murder," she informed him with a shudder, the word autopsy in connection with her father unsettled her.

"Was there an investigation?" he wondered aloud.

"Yes, it's still ongoing, but so far there is no proof of exactly what happened," she admitted, "either from the police or from the private investigator I hired."

"Does your father really have seven sons?" He wanted to change the subject.

"Only four are really his sons, three are stepsons. He loved them all."

"What are your stepsisters like? In your world?"

"Thoughtless, jealous of me, but not evil. If they were away from Gertrude, I think they would be decent women. A bit dim, perhaps, and lazy but decent. Hiding my gowns seems to be one of their childish pranks, typical, even in my real life."

"What do you think of your father sending a royal decree with his wishes, in case something happens to him?"

"Something has him worried, and I know what or who that would be. I just hope he did enough to protect himself, but I fear he did not."

Chapter Ten

Snow White

As the morning passed, Snow excused herself from her father and went in search of a more suitable gown. Finding none, she shrugged philosophically. It didn't matter what she wore because she was not interested in the visiting Prince, she was just enjoying being with her father again.

She spent the afternoon strolling in the gardens and stitching some needlepoint. She also ran errands and did a few simple chores for Gertrude and her two stepsisters. It seemed all three of the women wanted to keep her busy.

She never saw Prince Robert. From time to time during the day she heard a low voice, masculine and warm, punctuated by shrill feminine laughter, but she never actually saw the man.

Her first glance of the visiting Prince was at dinner when she sat in her chair and looked up into the most extraordinary blue eyes she'd ever seen. She found herself staring at his face.

He was a classic example of male perfection. He had a strong chiseled face, with a square, firm jaw. Snow found herself glad that no beard was covering that jaw. He also had a straight nose, high cheekbones and his skin was smooth and unmarred, but not soft. His lips looked full and firm, and when he smiled his teeth were gleaming white. His eyes were a brilliant blue. He had thick expressive brows over those wonderful eyes; eyes that normally held humor and intelligence but seemed bewildered at the moment. His hair was black, shiny, and tied back into a queue at the nape of his neck.

He was dressed simply, in a black tunic shot through with threads of gold, and black tights. The tunic could not conceal the strength of his chest and arms, the tights could not even begin to conceal the muscles in his legs. Unfortunately for all the women in the room, his tunic was long enough to cover the bulge of his crotch.

Snow felt her heart beating rapidly in her chest. She felt instantly alive in a way she had never been before. It was like a dream, or a fantasy. She had never been prone to flights of fancy, but at that moment she saw stars in the depths of his eyes. She saw the wonder of new snow and a crisp winter's day in his smile. She heard the music of love in his voice.

She gave a small gasp as she felt a strange shiver run down her spine. Her legs suddenly felt weak. Her breasts seemed to tingle, they felt heavy and somehow fuller. She dropped her eyes and struggled to hide her reaction to the man, but she knew in that instant, her life had changed forever. She had awakened to passion, love, even lust in that one quick glance.

So when he was introduced to her by her father with a courteous, "My dear, may I introduce Prince Robert. Prince Robert, my daughter, Princess Snow," she froze, too taken aback to speak.

The Prince reached out to clasp her hand. All she could manage was a muttered, "Charmed." Her hand tingled where he touched it.

"Likewise," the Prince said in the same hushed tone before bending low to kiss the back of her hand.

Neither the Prince nor Snow met each other's eyes. If she had even taken the slightest glimpse into his eyes, she would have seen the stunned expression on his face. If Snow had been just a bit older, or more sophisticated, she would have recognized the naked desire in his voice. She did not have that experience, did not see his eyes, so she was unaware that his reaction to her matched hers to him. Not at the introduction, or during the wine before dinner, or even at dinner itself.

They did not have their dinner in the great hall that evening, but instead in the smaller, more elaborate family dining room. The great hall was still filled with the King's men, Prince Robert's entourage and various castle inhabitants.

The family dining room held only the King, Gertrude, Bridget and Bianca, Princess Snow and Prince Robert. Servants attended to their every need. The wine and ale flowed freely and so did the conversation. Her father and the Prince discussed finances, military concerns, and caring for the peasants. Bianca discussed the rose garden with the Prince. And discussed it, and discussed it, ad nauseam.

Bridget discussed women's fashions with the Prince, or rather she tried to, but the Prince had no interest at all in women's fashions. Her stepmother, Gertrude, stole the show, however. She was in on every conversation, turning every subject under discussion back to herself. Her outrageous bids for attention were embarrassing. She leaned over to speak to the Prince in an obvious ploy to get him to notice her bosom. No one could fail to notice her outlandish behavior, not even Snow, who was so smitten with the Prince that she couldn't speak a single word. Snow was silent but she was still observant. She was also very angry for her father's sake and humiliated for the Prince.

Needless to say, dinner was a disaster.

After dinner the Prince asked Snow to take him for a walk in the garden. Ignoring the uproar the simple request caused, with protests coming from everyone except the King, she agreed. The Prince rose and walked over to Snow, and with a courtly bow, took her hand and led her out the side door to the garden.

Behind her, she heard Gertrude's strident voice, "Well, I never!"

"That's true, my dear," the King replied with ominous quiet in his voice. "You have never acted so disgracefully in front of a guest before. You are a married woman, however much you would like to forget it, and much older than he is, at that. You could be his mother. You embarrassed both myself and our guest with your outright wantonness. I brought the man home in hopes that he would take an interest in one of our daughters, but you were so enamored of him that you would have cut out your own two children in your quest for his attention. You are a disgrace and on the morrow, I will have my men move you to your dowager estates. I no longer can abide your presence in this castle!"

"You cannot!" Gertrude protested. "You will not." Her eyes narrowed. "You dare not!"

"I can. I will," the King replied coldly. "And I do so dare. Do you dare question my orders?"

"Your Highness!" Bianca asked loudly, "What about us?"

"'Tis your choice. Stay or go," the King told Bianca. He looked over to meet Bridget's eyes. "Either one of you. I care for you both, but I will not stand for behavior like your mother's in this castle again. I was in hopes that the Prince would be attracted either to one of you or to Snow. I think he would be a good match for one of my daughters. I never expected my own wife to try to make an illicit match with him while I was in the room. If he doesn't leave in disgust, mayhaps one of you can still catch his eye."

"Yea, Father, we will stay," Bridget said.

"There is one condition," the King said sternly. "You must be fair. The man must be free to make his own selection about who he would like to court."

"What are you saying?" Bianca asked slowly.

"Snow couldn't find any gowns in her wardrobe that were fitting to meet a prince in. All there was in her wardrobe this morning were childish skirts and blouses," the King said firmly. "I expect that on the morrow her gowns will be returned to her wardrobe and there will be no further tricks of that sort."

"Of course not, Your Highness," Bridget said with a quivering voice.

"Bianca?" the King asked.

"Yea, Sire," Bianca replied, resentment in her tone.

"My daughters, why are you so reluctant to give to me on this point?" the King asked with genuine concern in his voice. "I only want you to be fair to Princess Snow."

"My pardon, Majesty, but in being fair to Snow you put us at a great disadvantage. She has a certain beauty, with the quality of serenity added to go with it. Many a man would fall for her graces," Bridget said softly. "Bianca and I are, frankly, plain."

"Sister!" Bianca protested.

"'Tis true that Princess Snow has a certain beauty of face and form," the King said, "but so do you both. She has a pleasing nature. You are all different but each of you has your own special beauty, and I will help you both find excellent husbands if you let me. I want all three of my daughters to be happy."

The two girls, reassured, hugged the King. Gertrude, watching from the shadows, got even angrier. She was jealous of the affection her girls had for the King. She knew they had little real affection for her. She hated the King with every cell of her black heart. And she began to plot.

In the garden, Prince Robert led Snow to a low bench and sat beside her. Snow was still quiet, tongue-tied, and ill at ease. Even so, there was nowhere else she wanted to be. She was strangely and very strongly attracted to this beautiful man. It was not just his looks, she felt compassion and strength of character in him. She was gripped with the shock of finding love so quickly and unexpectedly. She knew, deep in her heart, that this was a real love, not just attraction to an extremely handsome man.

The Prince talked to her quietly, and slowly she began to open up to him. To her surprise, she found that aside from love, she truly liked the Prince. She knew her feelings came to her quickly before she knew aught of his character: his manner, his humor, his intelligence and compassion.

She was comforted to learn he was much more than a pleasing face and form, he was warm and funny and clever. That made it easier to like him and oddly, still harder to talk to him. Except for one thing, talking to him had become the most important thing in her world at the moment. So she overcame her maidenly shyness and opened her mind, as well as her heart to the handsome Prince.

"Tell me more about your home and your family," she asked the Prince. "You have seen mine already. What can I say about them?"

"My mother is a wonderful woman, warm and caring," the Prince told her. "She is very smart for a woman."

"For a woman?" For the first time, there was a hint of impatience in Snow's voice.

"I do know women have the same brains as men," the Prince hastily acknowledged, "but they use them differently. I know not why, but 'tis true. Look at your sisters; tonight one of them wanted only to discuss women's fashions with me. Do I look like I care about women's fashions?"

He smiled as he heard Snow give a small, unladylike snort. "The older one, what was her name? It matters not, she only wanted to discuss the rose garden. It was all she could talk about. 'Tis a beautiful garden, true, but what is there to discuss here? 'Tis a garden. 'Tis full of roses."

"And my stepmother made a fool of herself," Snow said softly. "Acting like the lowest strumpet before you. Not to mention myself."

"You did nothing wrong," the Prince said. "I found you to be totally charming."

"I was so enamored of your face and form that I could not speak," Snow softly confessed, blushing at the admission.

"And is it not wonderful that I was equally enamored of everything about you?" the Prince whispered back.

He looked into her eyes for a long, timeless moment. His head made a slight movement towards hers. Her face tilted to meet his. Millimeter by millimeter the distance between their faces closed, their lips slowly but surely approaching each other's.

"Snow!" she heard her father call. "'Tis time for bed."

They both pulled back in surprise.

"Coming, Father," she called out, then turned reluctantly back to the Prince. "Goodnight, Prince Robert," she said softly, hiding her frustration.

She rose from the bench and started to go back to the castle. Suddenly she turned back to face him. "Will you still be here in the morning?"

"No, regretfully I have to leave. I have a very important message to take to my father," he told her reluctantly. "I will return soon, very soon. I have a great need to be here, near you."

"I will miss you until you return." She held out her hand to him and blushed as he kissed it courteously.

Both of them hid the rush of passion that rushed through each of them at that small kiss on the back of her hand.

"I will return soon, as soon as possible," he said once again softly. "If you have a need for me, send a message with one of your father's trusted men."

Once inside the house, Snow hugged her father tightly and kissed him goodnight. She said, "Father, have I told you oft enough that I love you?"

"You have told me oft, and I know it well," he smiled down at her, stroking her hair, "but it can never be oft enough. I love hearing those words from you, my daughter, just as I love you."

Snow went up to her chamber. She laid herself on her big feather bed and gently touched her lips. In wonder, she thought about the kiss that almost just happened. She remembered the look on his face as he had moved closer to her, how she knew he clearly intended to kiss her. She was an innocent young woman but she knew she had seen the passion in his eyes, intent in his manner. She wondered what he would have said. What would it have been like? She knew instinctively that it would have been such a kiss as dreams are built on. How she wished that kiss had happened. How she yearned for that kiss, her first real kiss. When she finally fell asleep, she dreamed of the Prince and in her dreams, at least, he did kiss her, a long, soft, romantic kiss. She sighed, even in her dreams.

"So once again I'm Prince Robert?" He was amused.

"It seems that way, as you were in the other story. It makes me wonder, were you a prince in the highlands?"

"I was not a prince but I was the heir to the McDougal, in line to be the head of the clan," he explained.

"So you were important in your clan. It sounds very much like a prince. How did you come to be under a witch's spell?" That had been puzzling her.

"I had a cousin who was jealous of my position. He pressured the witch to make a poison to kill me, but she was a good woman and had no heart for murder. She was one of my most trusted friends. She did make something that seemed to be poisonous, I looked dead but I was not, not really. She put a spell on me but left me a way out. That's why I have to find love in the land of shadows." He sounded grim as he remembered his cousin's treachery.

"Why did she not go to your family? Or warn you? Or do something to save you?" Cyn couldn't understand.

"Dauid, my cousin, had kidnapped her young daughter and threatened to kill the child. She was terrified," he explained. "I do know that Dauid was killed shortly after I entered the land of shadows, but the witch could not reverse the spell."

"Did she even try?" Cyn prodded.

"Yes. She has also stayed with me, here," he said softly. "She has helped me."

"How?"

"Well, most recently, she was your fairy godmother." He grinned.

A sudden realization hit Cyn. "She also seems to be my housekeeper."

Chapter Eleven

Snow White

Not long after the Prince's visit, Snow's father urged her to ride out with him as he went hunting. He knew she was missing the Prince, and though he was sympathetic to her plight, he was also pleased. It seemed the two had fallen in love which was something he and Prince Robert's father had long wanted. Snow knew there was little to do in the castle except chores for Gertrude, who continued to treat her as a servant when Snow's father was not around, so she agreed to go on the hunt. Her mare was saddled for her and she rode out with her father and his men as he went hunting.

Although she took no joy from shooting animals, she was practical, she knew full well it was how her food got on the table. She loved being with her father outside the castle, without Gertrude around. She truly enjoyed the ride and the gallop through the woods, urging her mare to jump over some logs.

She pulled her mare up and turned to her father. "Sire, are you really sending Gertrude away?"

"Yea, Snow," he said sadly. "I had such hopes when I married her but I can no longer stand to have her in the castle. She is trying to get me to let her stay but I will not. I gave her time to pack and say farewell to her few friends. She has but a fortnight left to leave, or my soldiers will escort her away by force."

They started to ride again. They had ridden quite a fair distance from the castle. The King forgot his frustration with Gertrude and was enjoying the hunt. He brought down a stag. His guards were also hunting, and several of them were after a wild boar. Suddenly an arrow struck the King square in the chest and he fell from his horse. It was swift, unexpected, and deadly.

Snow screamed, "Father!" and leapt from her horse.

She never knew it, but that leap saved her life, as an arrow shot past her and struck a tree near her head. Her full attention was focused on the unbelievable sight of her father lying still on the ground with blood gushing from his chest and the arrow sticking out. She screamed for help as she tried in vain to staunch the flow of blood, tears running down her cheeks. She knew and fought the knowledge, that her efforts were too late, her attempts to save him were futile. He was as good as dead the instant the arrow struck him, even if he did manage to grasp her hand and mumble one word: "Love."

The guards came, some running and some riding to her, surrounding her even as she knelt by her father, each had their bow drawn and an arrow notched. Once they reached her, she collapsed in grief.

The head guard gently picked her up and cradled her as she cried. She never saw the tears running down his own rugged cheeks. "Your Highness, please, let me help you."

"Who would have done such a thing?" she choked out. "Was it an accident? It seems so but..."

"I do not believe it," he said to her. "We will find out who did this and make sure the culprit tells us who is truly behind this. They will all pay with their lives."

"I know who the true culprit is," Snow managed. "As do you."

"Aye, Princess Snow," his reply was soft but grim. "We know but we need proof."

He ordered one of the mounted guards to put her on his horse, in front of him, and carry her back to the castle with two more guards protecting her, and one leading her mare. Then he assigned his best men to carry the body of the King back with all the respect and dignity he deserved. He left a few of his best hunters to search for signs of the villain who had shot the King.

They found a dead man, with his throat cut, not far from the place where the King had fallen, with an excellent sight for aiming at the King. He knew the man to be an excellent archer with low morals. Evidently once the man had made the shot, his value was over and he had become a liability. Except for his brief comment to Snow, the guard kept his thoughts about who was behind the assassination to himself until he could find proof. He found the second arrow in the tree, near where Snow would have been beside the King. Furious, and working to cover his anger, he rode at a gallop to catch the men escorting the body of the King to the castle.

When the guards arrived back at the castle with the King's body, he sent the stable boy for Gertrude. When she appeared, he informed her coolly of the assassination of the King. She met his eyes with disdain, no trace of surprise or mourning.

Gertrude immediately began to call herself Queen Gertrude, and act as the Queen assuming authority many knew she was never meant to have. One of her first acts as queen was to hire more guards, men loyal only to her and willing to fight dirty.

Snow was so grief-stricken that she took to her bed where she sobbed out her grief, then went silent, not speaking or responding to anything. Her priest visited her daily but she barely responded to his presence. She hardly ate. She stayed in her chamber, in bed. Her only grooming was done by her maid, who bathed her and combed out her hair. It was eerie for the maid who felt as if she was working on a corpse. Snow slept much of the time and slowly the sleep began to restore her. She would wake for short periods, talk a few words to her maid, eat a bit, then sleep again. Once, when she woke, she asked her maid to bring the head guard to her. She gave him a message for Prince Robert and asked him to see it was delivered.

One day shortly thereafter, she seemed almost cheerful for several hours. She rose and groomed herself, talking quietly to her maid. She even went down to the parlor and talked to her stepsisters. When Gertrude entered the room, however, she fell silent, rose and returned to her room, sinking back into a deep and troubled sleep.

Her stepmother and two stepsisters reacted to the King's passing somewhat differently than Snow had; they grieved publicly, then promptly opened her father's coffers and bought new gowns and shoes. Their behavior had no effect on Snow's grief. She was desolate.

Since her father's untimely death, which occurred almost a month since the Prince's visit, Snow had noticed little that went on around her. She had forgotten much that had happened recently. She remembered that her precious father was dead, murdered right in front of her eyes. She also had her memories of Prince Robert. They had spent so little time together that the memories seemed more like romantic fantasies, filled with longing. During that time everything in the castle had changed forever.

The atmosphere in the castle, which had once been a happy place, was now bleak and dreary. Everyone, down to the lowest servant, seemed sadder and more subdued than before. They could be seen moving slowly with a heavy tread, their heads down and traces of tears in their eyes. In spite of their elaborate spending, Bianca and Bridget seemed to mourn her father sincerely. They treated Snow with a new care. Their kindness and support were the only bright spots in the whole tragic situation for Snow. They both offered her a surprising amount of sisterly concern and comfort. They shared her grief with her and supported her, freely offering their sympathy and love. She was touched by their show of genuine affection for her father.

Outwardly, the King's death was barely questioned. The King's own guards investigated his death, but they found nothing to tie it directly to the Queen. They said it was a hunting accident. They said they would probably never find out who had hired the archer who shot the arrow. But in truth, the guards were not satisfied with the King's death. They knew full well it was no accident, and they said so amongst themselves. The King's second wife was probably behind it, they said, but only did so in a whisper.

Tension filled the castle. Snow tried to stay away from the intrigue and danger but she failed to avoid it completely. One night as she walked down the staircase, she felt hands on her back, pushing her. Whoever gave her that push was tentative and that saved Snow's life. The push made her stumble and fall to her knees, but it was not hard enough to cause her to fall to her death. A passing guard ran to her aid and the page who had pushed her was caught.

The lad, only about twelve, was pale, his freckles standing out on his face. Tears were forming in his eyes. Snow followed as the guards led him out of the castle to the stables.

"Seth, why did you push me?" Snow asked him softly. "I could have been killed."

"I was told to!" The tears streamed openly down his face. "I was ordered to kill you with a push down the stairs."

"Why did you follow those orders?" Snow insisted. "Have I not always treated you well?"

"Yea, Princess, but my younger sister was taken. She's missing." He sobbed. "I got a message that either I kill you or my younger sister would be killed! She is only ten. Believe me, I did not wish to harm you, Princess Snow."

Snow studied his face, seeking signs of treachery, seeking the truth. "I believe you."

"Hide him here and seek out his family." She turned to the head guard. "Find his sister and return her to her family."

She met with the head guard in the stables. She paced in a small circle as she gave him instructions. "Give out the word that I have fallen and may not live, make a show of carrying me to my chambers, then make sure the lad's family is safe and send them all over to Prince Robert, with my request that they are to be protected."

"Including him?" the guard asked. "He should be punished."

"Yea, including him, he's but a lad who was in a desperate place," Snow said firmly. "I will remain in my chambers until his family is safe."

"Strange," the guard murmured as he watched Snow walk away, "the Queen usually makes a better choice for her tool. She must be desperate."

Snow's stepmother had seized control and declared herself to be Queen. Queen Gertrude was in charge of everything and ran the kingdom with an iron fist. Although there were murmurs and suspicions no one could find proof that she was not following the late King's dying wishes.

There was a strong belief that the King would have wanted Snow to follow him as Queen Snow, but the new Queen produced a writ that named her as the King's heir and successor. The King's guards doubted the authenticity of the writ and kept searching for proof that it was false.

They were also looking for ways to place the blame for the King's death on the Queen, but they did it hampered by the need to keep their inquiries away from her attention. Inexorably the rumor that the Queen was behind the murder of the King crept through the castle.

The decree the King had told Snow about was never found. She was in such turmoil that she had forgotten what her father had said about sending a copy of it away for safekeeping. He had never finished telling her where he had sent the copy and who was taking care of it for him anyway. As for the Queen's writ, most of the inhabitants of the castle knew well how he despised the woman, and believed the document to be false, but they were quickly silenced, some permanently.

Gertrude almost ran the country to ruin with her extravagances. She would not listen to any advice. If someone offered it to her she would shriek, "Silence! Silence! Silence!" at the top of her lungs, all sign of nobility and decorum forgotten. Sometimes she even beat on the table as she shrieked. She was also getting fearful. She was paranoid, thinking all those around her were plotting against her. Her paranoia had a real basis in fact. She was both ruthless and rude. She was also hated.

"Off with his head!" seemed to be one of Queen Gertrude's favorite sayings.

Snow was submerged in her grief, unaware of the rumors and all the intrigue swirling around her. The suspicions about the King's death and the Queen's involvement were growing but Snow was so inconsolable that the rumors and gossip about her father's death escaped her notice until one of the guards hinted it to one of the buxom, young housemaids on the sly, looking over his shoulder, terrified of being overheard. Neither of them noticed Snow as she almost was about to enter the room. Snow backed away, shaken to the depth of her soul. Soon after telling the maid about the rumors, the guard was atop her on the floor of the kitchen pantry and he forgot all about dire plots.

After hearing the talk between the horny guard and the maid, Snow gradually began to wonder and to remember that last private conversation with her father the night Prince Robert first came to visit.

The memory brought some questions to the forefront of her mind. She began to take long walks in the garden and even in the surrounding woods, the dark, mysterious woods. She constantly replayed her father's words of last year. Had he seen his own death coming? They were burning in Snow's mind but she could find no proof. Was he warning her to be wary of Gertrude? Was the guard right? Was Gertrude really capable of murder?

The questions brought Snow through her grief. She felt her sorrow fading and in its place, she felt anger and a growing desire for vengeance. Wisely, Snow kept her own council but pondered these questions as she went on with her daily life. She was biding her time; to find out the truth and if need be, reveal Gertrude for the evil woman she truly was, and to take her revenge. Few in the castle knew of the resolve and courage housed in her seemingly meek and delicate body, in her calm nature and innocent soul. They rejoiced in her recovered spirits, without knowing what brewed inside her. Outwardly she mourned quietly. Deep inside she was seething with rage.

She also remembered what her father had said about the next kingdom so she sent a trusted maid with a message to the stables, summoning her father's most trusted guard. Snow sounded him out about her father's death. The man admitted that he had his doubts about who was behind her father's murder but had no real proof. Snow told him about the conversation she'd had with her father during the Prince's visit the year before. What she said had the ring of truth to the guard; he knew that despite her youth, the old King would have wanted his daughter to succeed him.

"Oh my God!" Cyn felt the grief overwhelm her. "She had him killed. I knew it, in every life. Why couldn't I save him?"

"It was not to be." Robbie was sad, but resigned to the vagaries of fate.

"I can't stop thinking that if I could save him in Snow's reality, I could save him in my reality." She knew in her heart that was not true, but she could not shake the feeling.

"I cannae be sure, lass, but I do not think that is how it is meant to be." He hugged her mentally.

"I feel as if I should have known, I should have done something to protect him." She felt sad and frustrated.

"I suspect that until your father died you simply did not see the evil inside her," he told her.

"I knew she was rotten, in fact, I hated her." She was vehement.

"But you do not have the evil in you to kill. It is simply not something you would ever think of, but she would. That is why it was so hard for you to see." He tried to reason with her though he agreed with her.

"I have thought of it now. I could kill now." She paced, bitterness coming through in her voice.

"I know, Cyn, but you will not take that path. You could kill to save yourself or protect others, but for this? Nay, you would seek justice through the law." He was sure of that.

"You're right. I want her exposed and humiliated. I want her hunted, and I want her tried in a court and convicted. I want her to spend years locked up, either for life or waiting to be executed."

"Can you forgive her?" he wondered.

"I have to, by my faith." She paused. *"But that does not mean I do not want her to face the penalties for her actions. I can't do it until she is caught and tried. I can't forgive her if she's not facing any consequences. Does that make any sense?"* She made her feelings clear.

"Yes, it does, and of course, you cannot forgive her while she is still free to try to have you killed."

"Oh my God!" she said suddenly. *"I must go back to my body, something is happening!"*

They watched as the doctors worked on her, one shouting, *"Clear!"* as her body jerked in shock.

"What is happening?" he asked.

"My heart stopped," she explained. *"They are shocking it to start it again."*

They watched in tense silence as the doctors got her stabilized again. Both frightened, then both relieved.

Chapter Twelve

Snow White

Snow had instructed the guard to go to the next kingdom to speak with the King. She knew Prince Robert's father was a true friend of her father's so the more she thought about it, the more it seemed to her that he would be the one her father had entrusted with his decree. She wanted her man to carry a message from her telling him what had happened, and about her suspicions, and asking for the King's advice and assistance.

Many of those who were the closest and the most loyal to her father were gone, some having been quickly replaced by the Queen with new servants who were loyal to her. Others had simply been taken to the dungeon. Some, and no one knew how many, had lost their heads.

Even through her grief, Snow could not help but notice something strange about the new servants. The new female servants were all very plain, many well past their prime, and dressed in ugly, unflattering clothes. The new male servants were all young and very handsome of face. They all had muscular builds and tight, form-fitting uniforms that seemed to show off their broad chests, strong arms, and firm, taut behinds. Snow also couldn't help noticing their lack of intellect, their viciousness, or their fierce loyalty to Gertrude, who had declared herself Queen. Several of them spent an inordinate amount of time alone with the Queen in her chambers.

The Queen had even begun redecorating the castle, replacing some of the rich, tasteful appointments with gaudier, flashy things like paintings, tapestries, vases, and most notably a very large, gilt mirror hanging in her bedchamber. Gertrude seemed to grow more selfish and vain with each passing day. Much of her time was spent in front of the ornate mirror in her chambers, staring into it and muttering. Indeed, there seemed almost to be a trace of evil or insanity in her vanity, and she seemed to grow ever more resentful of Snow's youth and innocent beauty. Her antagonism to Snow made it easy for Snow to come and go as she wanted. The only time Gertrude wanted Snow around was to give her chores and belittle her.

Snow was so saddened by the changes in the atmosphere around the castle, the overwhelming gloom surrounding the place without her father there, that she often had to escape. It was easy. Gertrude did not want her around. If the new Queen was reluctant to give Snow leave to go, for some reason, Snow merely kept close to her until the Queen sent her away in annoyance. Freed, Snow either rode one of her horses, her mare or her gelding, or she took long walks in the woods, for she loved the birds and creatures she saw there.

Prince Robert had been back to visit many times since meeting Snow, but she was never allowed to see him. Either she was kept sequestered in her chambers when he was around, as were her two stepsisters, or sent away from the castle entirely.

Usually, when Gertrude made things so unbearable, she went to see her brothers. She had to be cautious since the boys were hidden from Gertrude, but she did find ways to visit them. Their caretaker was excellent, very attentive and completely loyal to the late King and Snow. He truly loved the boys. They were given chores and lessons but they were a cheerful bunch, filled with songs and laughter, even whistling. The boys were always pulling pranks on each other, their teacher, and even Snow.

Once they rigged a bucket of water to fall on their teacher when he opened the door, laughing at him while he stood there dripping and furious. They constantly had minor fights with each other. Fights that were forgotten in minutes. It was always hard for Snow to leave their small home and return to the castle because she longed to have them living in the castle with her. She vowed to herself that one day when it was safe, she would make it so.

One day, as usual, she went out riding to escape the gloom of the castle. She found a quiet spot and dismounted. She led her gelding over to the stream and let him have a drink, then tied him to a tree. She sat down on a hollow log and relaxed, relieved to be free of the pressures and intrigue of the castle.

She sang sad songs remembering her father and sweet songs about her future when she was grown up enough to find the love of a handsome prince. She had oft napped under such a tree and daydreamed about the Prince she would find, indeed believed she had already found.

In her daydreams, he always looked like Robert. Also, in her daydreams, she was not shy and tongue-tied. In these dreams, she told him what was in her heart and he shared his heart and dreams with her. They were meaningful, sincere and touching conversations in her daydreams, but they were innocent, not passionate. Even in her dreams, Snow did not go that far, she simply did not know what passion was.

Unknown to Snow, Prince Robert often watched Snow from the cover of the woods. He loved watching her as she walked through the woods singing. She had a soft, pleasing voice that could charm the birds from the trees. Literally. Of course, the handful of grain she often held out, standing there singing so softly, probably helped. On one occasion, a young fawn even approached her as she sat under a tree. Reaching into her pocket she pulled out another handful of grain and held it out to the young deer.

The fawn nibbled delicately at the grain before turning to leap away. Instinctively, Snow followed and found out why the fawn was out walking around without its mother. The doe was injured, with an arrow through its leg. She could stand, but barely walk. The animal was weak from the injury, slowly dying, and suffering from lack of water, the pond being too far away for her to get to it.

Prince Robert watched in amazement as she spoke gently to the animal, pulling a knife out of her pocket and cutting the end off the arrow. With gentle hands and easy motions, she pulled the arrow out of the doe, who seemed to instinctively trust her. Then she pulled something more out of her pocket, a small pouch filled with a pungent potion, which she spread on the doe's injury. Using a soft leather flask she carried she gave the doe a small drink. It wasn't enough, but it seemed to enliven the gentle creature.

Gently, step by step, with infinite patience, she led the animal to the nearest stream so the doe could really drink her fill. After that, when she walked in the woods, the doe and her fawn were often nearby. They never approached her so closely again, but walked alongside her, watching from the cover of the brush. Just as Robert did. He often saw them as he watched Snow. He held back, for some instinctive reason, not making his presence known to her.

At dinner one night, several months after her father's death, Snow's stepmother had some exciting news. It seemed Prince Robert, from the next kingdom, was coming back for yet another visit. It seemed strange for Gertrude to be so excited about the visit since her daughters knew he had been a guest at the castle several times. She even hinted that the Prince, a handsome man of barely twenty years, might be seeking a bride. Gertrude giggled and blushed like a young maiden when she said that.

Blanche and Bianca were both atwitter with the wondrous news, but it was Queen Gertrude who was the most excited. She forgot her age in her exaggerated sense of self-worth and greatly overrated and fading beauty. She was not a young woman. Indeed, she had two daughters in their mid-twenties. Her once famous looks had long since begun to weaken, but she still thought the Prince was coming for her.

Aloud, Snow wondered how excited one was supposed to get over a man she'd barely met, the royal Prince or not. Deep inside, she was thrilled on two levels. First, her heart leapt at the thought of seeing the Prince again. She remembered the way she had felt upon first seeing his face, looking into those eyes. How they had talked in the garden and how he had almost kissed her. Also, she hoped that her message to his father had prompted this visit. God willing, there was some support for her to use against the treacherous Queen.

The notice of the latest visit by the Prince caused quite a stir around the castle. It seemed he planned a longer visit this time, staying for almost a fortnight. Preparations caused a real upheaval in the routine of the castle. Rooms were cleaned and aired out. Massive quantities of food were prepared. New clothes were made for Gertrude, Blanche, and Bianca, expensive gowns of the richest silks and satins. Gertrude's gowns were very daringly cut and trimmed with the finest jewels and most luxurious furs. Blanche and Bianca both got new gowns although not so expensively trimmed and certainly with less décolletage. As usual, Snow did not get a new gown.

Two days before the Prince was due to arrive, Snow was sitting in the great hall, not doing anything, just sitting quietly. A servant brought her a platter of meat and cheese. She nodded her thanks, although she had no appetite. Absently she sat there, thinking and feeding bits of the meat to some of the castle dogs. She was so lost in her thoughts that she paid no attention to her surroundings. Finally, she decided to eat a bit of the meat herself.

"Princess Snow!" She heard the head guard call out in alarm just as she cut off a small bit of the meat for herself. "What has happened to the dogs?"

Snow looked down and gasped in horror. Two of the castle dogs lay nearby, dead, and a third was gasping, struggling to breathe. There was a small patch of vomit near his mouth. "I... I was not hungry so I fed them some of the meat I was brought."

Even as she said it, the third dog died. She shuttered to see the guard use a knife to dispatch a fourth.

"He was getting ill," the guard said brusquely. "The meat was poisoned. The dogs saved your life."

"But who?" Even as she asked, she knew.

"I'll question the servant who brought you the food, but 'tis likely she's innocent in this," he said, eyeing her and pondering her nerve. "I will have the guards warned, the old guards, not hers."

"I will have to be watchful and careful." Snow shivered then visibly straightened her spine. "The Queen wants me dead."

"Aye, lass." He nodded approving of her nerve. "That she does. I vow she will be disappointed. We should have known. There was an arrow that almost hit you when your father was shot. In all the confusion, we thought it might have been an accident."

"Well, now I'm forewarned," Snow said firmly. "And I'm no easy target. I'm young but I'm good with a bow and also with a sword. You trained me yourself."

"There is one thing she has, lass, that you do not. She has evil in her soul." He snarled. "But you have something she does not know about."

"What's that?" Snow asked.

"You have a group of very loyal guards who truly love you, who are watching you. We honor your father and could not protect him. It will not happen again. We are willing to a man to die for you. She has men who work only for money. They have no real loyalty." With conviction the old guard said, "We will keep you safe."

"If she catches you protecting me you will be in great danger," Snow warned him, filled with pride and gratitude at his words. "Do not lose your heads."

"The men I pick to guard you would gladly die for you, Your Highness," he said once again. "We failed your father and he was a great man, but we will not fail you, my true Queen."

She bowed her head to him, and at that moment she truly looked and felt like a queen. She knew, in that instant, that she was in a war to the death with Gertrude. Maybe Prince Robert would come to her aid, but for now, she was alone, with only her guards to rely on. Suddenly the wait for his arrival seemed endless.

"So you watched me in the woods?" She was incredulous.

"Many times. Watching you was one of my favorite pastimes. I saw you heal the doe," he admitted then pointed out, "you also have some men you can trust, brave and loyal guards."

"I wish I had known you were there. I've felt so lonely lately, I mean Snow." Cyn identified with Snow, was Snow at that moment.

"I thought it best to see what I could of the intrigue in the castle. I knew you were well guarded."

"I know. I do trust my guards, at least the ones who've been here since my father was alive. The new guards? No, they are Gertrude's. They were hired for two reasons: utter viciousness and loyalty to Gertrude. Of course, they are also what we now call eye candy." She grinned.

She heard his laughter as she faded once more into sleep.

Chapter Thirteen

Snow White

Finally the big day arrived, the lookout in the tower spotted the Prince and his guards approaching the castle. He sounded a trumpet to let the Queen know the Prince was approaching. Almost everything was ready but, as always, there were last minute details to be quickly taken care of.

A lavish feast was prepared. Roast game birds were baked into elaborate pies and a side of beef was prepared. Sumptuous sauces were made and placed to complement every dish. There were fruits and cheeses, mouth-watering pastries, and all served with the finest selection of wines and ales. The table was set with all the best linens, the best silver, the finest goblets, and all were freshly polished to a high shine. Elaborate floral arrangements lined the table, and garlands were hung about the great hall.

As was usual for Queen Gertrude's new reign, the others in the castle were not so well served, and their meal was considerably less lavish. They did eat better than usual though, as Gertrude wanted even the Prince's entourage to be impressed.

Gertrude was dressed in her richest gown, a vibrant blue gown with an extremely low neckline, her over-sized bosom almost completely exposed. Every breath she took seemed to risk complete exposure. Her hair was piled high atop her head and powdered glaring white. Blanche and Bianca were also decked out in their finest, but they wore more modest necklines and their hair was done with less exaggerated height and left without powder.

Snow was once again in her usual girlish gown, with her long hair merely tied back with a silken ribbon. She felt childish and awkward. Although she was seventeen, she was given children's clothes as her usual wardrobe since the death of her father because even Gertrude realized she was extremely beautiful. Dressed in stylish clothes, she would be a real rival.

Gertrude failed to realize that even dressed as a child, Snow had a freshness and an innocent beauty that would move almost any man to care for her. Almost any man would want to protect her, worship her. The only reason Gertrude's own daughters got fancy, stylish gowns was that Bridget and Bianca could wear fancy gowns and they would still be plain and somewhat unattractive.

Finally, the arrival of the young Prince Robert was announced, and Gertrude went forward to greet him. Gertrude flirted outrageously with the young, handsome Prince, barely taking time to formally acknowledge him to her daughters, Blanche and Bianca.

"And you may remember this child, my stepdaughter, Snow," she added ungraciously.

"Charmed, Princess Snow," the Prince said gallantly. A thrill went through him as their eyes met, leaving him feeling stunned. "'Tis good to see you again."

Snow was feeling equally stunned. Prince Robert certainly lived up her memories. She had half convinced herself that her memories were false, a way to ease the grief her father's death had imprinted on her mind. A pleasant diversion from her anger and pain. A memory made more intense because it was her first rush of passion. But it was not so, the Prince certainly lived up to the upheaval his arrival caused. He was indeed very handsome, tall, trim and fit. He also had very pleasing manners, courteous and friendly but not overly familiar.

The Prince was likewise enraptured with Snow. He had seen her many times, in the woods, but not spoken to her since the first visit. He knew, from the first heartbeat, that she would be his queen. He was a discreet young man, but he already knew the ways of passion and knew the rush of lust. This was different, the passion was there, as was the lust, but there was also something more, something timeless and true. With all he knew about recent events in the castle, he kept his feelings to himself and deliberately turned his attention to Gertrude.

He treated Gertrude with some warmth and also gave some of his attention to both of her daughters while limiting his interest in Princess Snow. He sat and conversed with the women over the evening meal. He noted Gertrude's blatant attempt to attract him and he was amused and amazed at her obvious flirting, but he was also put off by the outrageousness of her manner. In spite of her carefully structured glamour, there was something wrong about her, something sinister and menacing. Of course, she was also far too old to draw his interest; she had at least a dozen more years than did his own mother.

The two stepdaughters were also flirting but less obviously so. They were both even less attractive than he remembered. He was not one to judge a woman solely on her looks, but they both also seemed a bit dull and dim. Still, there was a hint of cunning in both, and an eye to their own advantage. However, he sensed no real malice in either of them. Indeed they seemed to show little interest in him, in spite of their mild flirting. They either realized that he was both too high born and also far too virile and handsome, or they were too afraid to cross their mother. Instead, they openly flirted with some of his guards.

All in all, he found the women of the castle barely interesting and certainly not alluring, but when he looked at Snow suddenly everything was different. She had a real beauty, the kind that would last long after her first blush of youth faded, and had an air of innocence and purity. She was also filled with sweetness and an inner warmth that made her special to many of the people in the kingdom, noble and peasant alike, both in and out of the castle. She had a joyous glow that had been muted since her father's death but seemed to be coming back to her in his presence.

The Prince was completely in love with Snow, touched by her quiet, gentle beauty and the carefully banked sadness that never completely left her eyes. He wanted to stay by her side and get her away from the castle and into his home. He wanted to make her smile again, really smile, not just a passing grin. He wanted to lie with her and hold her during long, cold nights, as well as in the full heat of summer. He wanted to teach her passion. He wanted her children to be his.

He was also smart enough to realize that the girl was considered a rival by Gertrude. He was aware that she was treated like a poor, lowly relative almost begging for crumbs in spite of the fact that she was also the true royal Princess, the one true daughter to the King. In fact, she was the only legitimate child of the King, and as such, his one real heir.

Gertrude and her daughters seemed to be ignoring the late King's proclamation naming Snow as his heir. In fact, she mentioned that she had a writ from the late King naming her his successor, claiming that he felt Snow was far too young to be Queen and questioning her knowledge and ability to rule the land.

Luckily the late King, Snow's father, had done exactly what Snow wished for. He had sent a copy of his true wishes, in the form of a proclamation to Prince Robert's father, along with a message outlining his distrust of Queen Gertrude. That was part of the reason he was there on a seemingly casual visit. He had been dispatched there to investigate the truth behind late King's message along with the second message, the one that had come from Princess Snow.

Prince Robert openly conversed with Gertrude and her two daughters, but he kept his notice of Snow under control. He was very aware of her every move. He noticed that, in spite of her childish clothes, she had a woman's curves, quite pleasing curves in fact. Her manner was gentle and kind, her smile warm and real. She treated the servants with patience, and her manner towards

Bridget and Bianca was caring and gentle. She seemed cool and reserved with Gertrude, but not openly hostile.

She excused herself early and went upstairs. He deeply regretted that he did not see her again that night. He sought a private moment with her, but he resigned himself to biding his time, although he was not known for exercising his patience.

Something happened the night after the Prince's visit ended, he later learned. It was something that would later make his patience come to a complete end. Something that would change how he dealt with Gertrude.

It happened this way: Snow intended to go to bed early. She had not eaten well during the Prince's visit. She could not stomach the sight of Gertrude flirting with Prince Robert. Part of it was the concern for her father's memory, but there was something else, too, something vague and disturbing. It was something she was not yet ready to face.

With the Prince gone, Snow was no longer forced to watch Gertrude's scandalous behavior. Her appetite returned. She stopped downstairs to grab a quick bite to take up to her bedchamber. Mayhaps away from Gertrude's flirting with the Prince, she could manage to eat. A few moments later, one of the Queen's maids appeared.

She drew Snow aside. "Begging your pardon, Princess Snow, but I wouldst speak with you, privately."

"What is the matter, Gwendolyn?" Snow asked gently.

"I wish to speak to you about the Queen," Gwendolyn said privately.

"She is not the Queen," Snow said in a quiet but vehement tone. "My father did not wish her to succeed him."

"I am truly sorry if I gave you any offense. I never knew your father. The Quee-, I mean Gertrude, brought me into her service after his death," the little maid said.

"Yes, she replaced many of the house servants and guards to rid the castle of those most loyal to the King," Snow told the girl.

"I may not have been in the castle long, and I may have no ties to the late King, your father, but I have heard much good of him. He was said to be a truly fine man," she said.

"I loved him well as a father and as a king," Snow said sadly, "and I miss him still."

"The new Quee-, I mean Gertrude, troubles me, Your Highness," Gwendolyn said.

"In what way?" Snow prompted.

"If she knew I had overheard her she would have me killed," Gwendolyn said, worried. "If I tell you I am in danger."

"What is it?" Snow prompted gently. "I will do all I can to protect you."

"Something is wrong with her. She talks to herself." Gwendolyn looked around, afraid to speak above a whisper.

"Talks to herself?" Snow pushed gently.

"In the mirror," the maid said softly. "She talks to herself in the mirror. She always has, but now she listens to it, as though it answers her. She asks the mirror if she is still fair and desirable to men. That is not new. She also asks it if she can make Prince Robert love her. She mentions ridding herself, in her words, of the late King. But what really scares me is that she sees you as a threat. I heard her asking the mirror what she should do about Snow."

"Thank you for coming to me, Gwendolyn." Snow felt a quick shiver run through her at the maid's words but remained outwardly calm. "I will be on guard against Gertrude. Once I rid the castle of her I will reward your for this service to me."

"Begging your pardon, Princess, but I believe you cannot win against her, not alone. She is too evil and far too cunning. I also believe she uses witchcraft because I have seen strange things that I think may be used in the dark arts." Gwendolyn asked, "Will her daughters help you?"

"They have no great love of their mother. I will approach them but I will be discrete," Snow said. "I think they will choose sides based on who they think will emerge victorious."

"I will not speak to you again unless there is further news," Gwendolyn said.

"I agree, 'tis too dangerous for you," Snow said. "Act as though you have not seen or heard anything unusual. Show her proper devotion as her servant. Try to avoid being around her when she is talking into her mirror."

"Yea, Princess Snow." The maid left.

The Queen, at first, had been relieved when Snow began spending so much time riding in the woods, but over time she changed her mind as she began to ask herself questions. Why was the brat spending so much time in the woods? Was she meeting with someone?

The Queen knew full well there were those in the castle who plotted against her. There were even those who believed she was behind the death of the late King. Even to herself she denied it, but they were right. What if they were meeting with Snow? Would they plot against her? Would they try to steal the crown she had stolen? It was hers!

There was another possibility with Snow's rides in the woods, what if she was to meet with Prince Robert? He was to be hers, not Snow's. She knew it, she had seen it in the mirror. She was so upset that she turned to her mirror with her questions, for once forgetting to make sure she was alone.

"Oh great mirror," she began, standing naked before the mirror, "Tell me if I am still the fairest in the land."

"I refuse to let you tell me my beauty is fading." She listened for a moment. "Am I not still young and fair?"

"You are supposed to help me get what I need, what I want." Her voice sounded normal, annoyed but normal. "I need Prince Robert, mirror, after all, I had the King murdered to get him. I tried to kill the brat Snow as well but my men have failed me three times. Two of the fools are dead and when I find the third, he will join them. Idiots! I shall have to kill the brat myself."

Gertrude whirled around as she heard a soft gasp. "Who is there?" she demanded in her strident voice. "Come out and show yourself! At once!"

She could not see who was there, hiding in the corner, but she heard a scuttling as whoever it was managed to get out the door. She threw on a robe and gave chase. She could not be sure who she was following but it was definitely a woman. Her guess was her foolish maid, Gwendolyn. She pulled on a robe and ran after the figure until she saw her trip and fall down the stairs.

Gertrude smiled, watching the figure tumble to the bottom of the staircase. As she watched the woman fall she knew it was indeed Gwendolyn. She saw several of the guards, the old guards still loyal to Snow and the late King, run to the aid of the still figure at the base of the stairs. Surely she was dead or would die soon. The important thing was that she did not speak before dying. Gertrude started down the stairs.

"I'm so happy you've come, Robbie. I needed you for your strength and support. I can feel you helping me, whether you know it or not, by easing my grief. I've been mourning so hard, I was putting myself in danger."

"Aye, lass, you have been. You have been mired so deep in mourning, you cannae see the dangers facing you," he agreed softly.

"Well, I am determined to end that and take note of what's going on around me. I want to live and to love. And, I want revenge." For once there was no mildness in her tone, instead it was filled with force and determination.

"Revenge?" He was not surprised.

"Well, justice," she admitted.

"Lass, you are right, she needs to be brought to justice. For your sake and for the boys you speak of." He paused. "There is one thing I must know, about that mirror. 'Tis not just vanity that has her staring into it and talking to it."

"No indeed, in the original tale it was a magic mirror but now I see

that is wrong." She paused. *"The mirror has no magic. Gertrude is quite simply mad. In my day, we'd say she has delusions or auditory hallucinations. And her madness? Her madness is that she has no sense of right and wrong or feelings for anyone but herself. She is what we call a sociopath. At least I think that's what they'd call it. I'm not trained in psychiatry."*

"Do not look at me, I do not even know what that is." He grinned in spite of himself.

"Oh my goodness!" Cyn was distracted. *"Gwendolyn fell down the stairs. I hope she's not hurt too bad. Was she pushed?"*

"No, Gertrude did not push her, but she was chasing her. She caused the fall as surely as if she did push her." His voice filled with anger.

"Snow must protect her now if she has any possibility of survival," Cyn declared. *"And with no modern medicine, her chances are slim."*

Chapter Fourteen

Snow White

Snow rushed into the great hall and knelt by Gwendolyn's side. "I can help her, Queen Gertrude, you need not trouble yourself," she called out. She then turned and nodded at one of her men and whispered, "Get rid of her lest she kill this poor girl."

"Your Majesty," the guard called up to Gertrude, "I was coming up to you when this poor thing fell. I have news that Prince Robert is on his way here. "'Tis said he is coming alone to court to find his future queen."

"I must get ready for him." Gertrude practically sang it, then called out, "Gwendolyn, you lazy chit, where are you?"

"Majesty, Gwendolyn is badly injured from the fall down the stairs. She may die," the guard reminded her.

In her vanity Gertrude had forgotten seeing the maid tumble down the stairs. "Well, no matter, fetch Bianca and tell her I need use of her maid. This is so inconvenient. Now I will need to find a new maid."

The guard went in search of Bianca and her maid.

Snow had her men gently carry Gwendolyn into a room off the great hall. She sent one of the men for her priest and another for the one who served as a healer in the castle.

Gwendolyn was moaning and muttering. Snow ordered the men, even the priest as he arrived, to listen to what she was saying but swore them to secrecy about what they might learn. "You must speak to no one about this except for Prince Robert or his father, the King, and his Queen mother. Tell anyone else the maid has died."

"The mirror... heard her tell mirror... she had him killed," Gwendolyn moaned, her voice barely above a whisper.

"Who did she order killed? Gwendolyn, who?" Snow asked her calmly.

"King, she wants Prince Robert," Gwendolyn struggled but got the words out.

Snow felt her fury rise inside her but kept calm outwardly; after all she already knew most of it.

Gwendolyn struggled to say one more thing, "Snow dead... wants Snow de-" She lapsed into a deep sleep.

"Is she dead?" one guard asked, his voice trembling just a little.

Snow looked at the guard, noting that he was younger than most, and saw the worried look in his eyes. She remembered that when Gwendolyn was falling he ran to try to save her. In fact, as she thought about it, she realized he had managed to catch her head and prevent her from slamming her head into the bottom step.

"No, she is not dead, but she is not yet safe," Snow told him. "She needs to be taken to Prince Robert's castle along with the priest and the surgeon. They need to go quickly, and in secret. The ride must be as smooth as possible. You take her and remain there. Tell the King what happened here today, and let him know we told Gertrude the Prince was coming to get her out of the way. He will know what to do."

"Aye, Princess." The young guard turned to leave.

Snow turned to her head guard. "Arthur, send Nyal and Walter with him, but they can return. They must move quickly and not let Gertrude know they were ever gone."

"And Liam can stay?" the guard asked, referring to the young guard.

"Yes, he loves her," Snow told him. "It shows."

"What will we do about Gertrude? Now she is expecting Prince Robert to come," Arthur asked, following Princess Snow's habit of not referring to Gertrude as the Queen unless she was present.

"She will be angered when he does not come." Snow thought for a moment. "Find a guard who has not been in the castle for a long time, and have him come dressed plainly, not in his guard clothes. Have him bring a message from the Prince telling her he was delayed and cannot come straight away. I will write it."

"Does she know your hand?" Arthur asked.

"No, I doubt it," Snow said slowly, thinking. "She is blind to that which does not concern her."

She quickly wrote:

> My dearest Queen,
> I regret that I am unable to come to you today as I had planned. Forgive me and know that I count the hours until I can see you once again.
>
> Your humble servant,
> Prince Robert

"Princess, she will be in a foul mood after receiving this, you must beware," Arthur warned her. "And if she learns you penned it, I fear for your life."

"She dare not kill me outright, too many in the castle are still loyal to my father and to me." Snow raised her chin in defiance. "And her attempts to have me meet with an accident have failed. I have to try."

"You will be well guarded," he assured her.

Unfortunately for Snow, Bianca was with the Queen when the note was delivered to her.

Without any ill intentions she took a quick look at the note and said, "Why is Snow writing you? Why does she not just speak to you?"

"Snow wrote this?" Gertrude asked with rising irritation. "Are you sure, girl?"

"It seems to be her penmanship, mother," Bianca replied.

Gertrude quickly summoned one of the new guards loyal to her and sent him into town with a message. She paced until the guard returned.

"Is he agreed?" she asked the guard.

"Aye, Majesty. He can have everything ready in three days," he told her. "He will come then."

"Go tell the servants to set our nightly dinner in the private dining room." Gertrude gave an evil smile.

Downstairs, Snow had just gotten the reports from Prince Robert. She was gratified to learn that Gwendolyn had survived the journey, although she was very badly injured. She had numerous cuts and her limbs were all sprained but seemed not to be broken. Snow was almost amused at the reports of her healer and his surgeon arguing over the maid's treatment. It seems the surgeon had some strange ideas, such as keeping the wounds as clean as possible, including washing his hands and his instruments. He also refused to bleed the girl, saying that part of her problem was the loss of blood, so how could bleeding help? He simply bound her wounds with herbs and used tight wrapping on her injured limbs. Neither of them knew of the potion Rosie had given the girl. To top it off, the two priests were praying so fervently that they kept getting in the way of the surgeon. Snow was hopeful as she got Gertrude's summons to dinner. However that optimism ended very quickly.

There was something wrong. Snow knew it as soon as she entered the room.

"Snow!" Gertrude greeted her with an unheard of enthusiasm, and her eyes were gleaming. "I have the best news for you."

Gertrude was positively glowing as she seated herself at the head of the table, the late King's place, Snow thought as she was filled with dread. Her stepsisters also took their places and wine was poured.

"Are you not going to ask me what my news is?" Gertrude asked Snow.

"No," Snow replied defiantly, "you are too excited. It cannot be good news."

"But it is," Gertrude insisted. "I have found a husband for you. You are going to be married, and very soon, in just three days. The bridegroom is very eager."

"Mama!" Bianca said urgently. "Why is Snow to be married before me? I am the oldest, I should be wed first!"

"She is to be married to a very wealthy and handsome man, Thomas the Earl of Greenwood," Gertrude said.

"Mama!" Bianca protested loudly. "He should be mine."

"You can be his next wife if you wish," Gertrude said in a brutal aside to Bianca, "since none of his four former wives survived more than a year with him. They all died from injuries that some say came from vicious beatings."

Snow gasped, afraid and horrified. "Even for you this is low, Gertrude."

"Queen Gertrude!" she shouted. "You will address me properly!"

"You are no Queen!" Snow shouted back. "You killed my father and have tried to kill me!"

Bianca and Bridget were stunned. They looked at each other, shocked beyond belief. Each of them liked Snow, but they both loved and feared their mother. They knew she had done some bad things, but this was too much for them to believe. This was evil. The two women were not dumb, and now they knew a battle was coming and they would have to choose sides.

"You will find out just how powerful I am as Queen and how ruthless I can be to my enemies," Gertrude shouted. "And no mistake, Snow, you are my enemy. I will crush you."

"You will only try, Gertrude," Snow shot back, all pretense at mild acquiescence gone and her full fury revealed. "You have failed to kill me three times. Each time you tried to kill me, more have rallied to my side. I have those standing with me you can only guess at. Before long I will take your place as Queen and you will be consigned to the dungeon. I swear it."

Snow ran from the room seeking someone, anyone, she knew to be loyal to her. The first person she came to that she could trust completely was her maid, but she was a delicate soul, not well suited for intrigue. She gave the maid a message, asking one of the cooks, Rosie, to come to her. She knew the cook and one of the stable hands were in love. She waited for Rosie to come and gave her a message to give to the stable hand, with instruction it then be given to the head guard far away from the castle.

In the note she told her guard what Gertrude had planned. The guard sent a message back through the stable hand to the cook to Snow. It was a simple message, not written down but given orally. It was only three words: Do not fear.

Gertrude waited excitedly for the earl to arrive, but when he was expected she got only a message that infuriated her. It seemed the earl had been brutally murdered by robbers on the way to the castle. She screamed her rage, then stormed into to her chambers and stood before her mirror.

Snow, when she heard Gertrude's scream of rage, did a brave but foolish thing. She hid herself in Gertrude's chamber and listened as Gertrude paced and raged at the mirror.

"Killed by highwaymen!" she screamed. "Nay! I do not believe it. Snow was behind it! I know it, great mirror. What can I do next?"

Gertrude paused, listening to the mirror which made no sound Snow's ears could detect. Gertrude hummed and nodded.

"It could work," she said. "With the potion, the Prince will do anything I say. He will be under my command completely just as her father was. The old fool. I will order him to kill Snow. It will be easy for him, the brat is enamored with him. First I have got to get him here, and while he is on the way I must make more of the potion. Thank you great mirror."

Gertrude left the room and Snow slipped out of her hiding spot, shaken to her very soul. This was no magic mirror that spoke to Gertrude! This was madness made stronger by pure greed and evil.

Snow made her way to the stables, intending to ride out. Riding was not only for pleasure when Prince Robert was not around, riding helped her work off her temper and think things through. The stable boy saw her coming. Acting on instinct he saddled her mare and got her ready to ride. The stable boy was a young lad loyal to Snow. Young as he was, he was wise to the ways of the world. He saw Snow's panic and confusion. He could not fail to notice how upset she was. He sought out her head guard without hesitation as soon as she galloped away.

"Sir, something is wrong with Princess Snow," he told the guard. "She was most upset when she took her horse out."

"Thank you, Thomas," he told the boy, "I will find her and learn what has her so upset. You did good to send for me."

"I am loyal to Princess Snow," Thomas said proudly then he grinned. "There is one more thing you should know. Lady Bianca has gone riding. She headed towards the lake."

"Lady Bianca hates horses and riding," the guard said firmly. "There must be a very strong reason to get her on a horse."

"One of the soldiers Prince Robert left here, Walter, rode that direction this morning as well," Thomas said knowingly, "and he seemed very happy."

"I will warn the Princess to ride in another direction," the guard said, "and find out if we can use this to our advantage. I know Walter is loyal to Prince Robert and the Princess."

The guard rode out to find the Princess. He was lucky and caught up with her before she got too close to the lake and warned her that Bianca was riding to the lake.

"Bianca on a horse!" Princess Snow exclaimed with a smile. "Why?"

"It seems, Milady, that she is meeting with one of the Prince's soldiers, a man named Walter. He is a good man."

"It must be love, nothing else would cause her to ride out." Snow smiled. "'Tis good."

"I hope I did not overstep my bounds, Princess, but I sent a message to Prince Robert a few days ago telling him there was intrigue at the castle," the guard said. "He should meet you at the river."

Snow's smile was enough to tell him that he had done the right thing. Still he needed to know what had her so upset that morning.

"Gwendolyn had told me Gertrude was talking to her mirror and listening to it as though it would answer her," Snow told him. "She said Gertrude talked about... about killing Father and trying to kill me."

"I suspected she was behind the murder of the King and the attempts on your life. I did not know about her speaking to the mirror. I am trying to prove her guilt and also to find out who she is using to do her dirty work. Finding the actual assassin dead in the forest was one thing, but it proved there was another working with him, the one who slashed his throat. That is all that has kept me from arresting her for treason and murder. My men would take her at my order," he told her, his anger showing through.

"Today I hid and listened to her and 'tis true, she seems to think the mirror talks to her," Snow told him. "She is mad, not just plain evil, but there is madness there as well."

"I have thought that as well. Does her madness excuse her evil?" he asked.

"No!" Snow said firmly. "Nothing excuses her evil. She wants to make a potion to give the Prince so he will do anything she wants. So he will marry her. I think it is how she got my father to wed her."

"Go find the Prince," the guard said. "I will make sure she is watched. She will make no potion to poison you or Prince Robert. I swear it."

"Let her make her potion," Snow suggested, "then replace it with something harmless."

Snow rode to the river, noticing that her mare seemed unusually fractious as she drew closer to the tree where she usually met the Prince. She soon found out why, as the Prince's stallion trumpeted at the mare. Snow jumped down from the mare and walked quickly to the Prince.

"Good day, Milady," he said softly as he gently took her hand. "I am very happy to see you."

"I am most happy to see you as well." Snow blushed as he kissed the back of her hand.

"Let us sit down by the tree and talk," he said. "From what I hear, there is much that needs to be said."

She looked at him in surprise. "From what you have heard? Do you have someone watching the castle?"

"I do indeed have several men watching the castle," he said softly, "to protect you, of course."

"I'm glad Gwendolyn has a chance to survive that fall."

"She has an excellent chance because your cook, Rosie, sent a potion with her. 'Twill help her heal."

"Rosie again?"

"Yes, she is a good witch, a great fairy godmother, an excellent cook."

"And a superb housekeeper. It took me a while to remember, I know, but I did have a bad injury. I've been in a coma, remember?" She laughed.

"No, really?" She felt his smile as he continued, "But is it not sad that your proposed bridegroom met with such a tragic fate?"

"Not at all," she smiled. "It is hard to grieve for someone I have never met."

"It is also hard to grieve for someone who has killed off every

woman he married, and some he merely took to his bed."

She had a phony smile. "Gee, I'm sorry I missed out on that. Gertrude has gotten more clever with this plan."

"What do you mean?" he asked.

"She is determined to see me dead. She's failed three times now: with the arrow, the fall down the stairs, and the poison. Now she wants to marry me off to a murderer? What's next? I pray that you, I mean the Prince, arrives in time to save me, I mean Snow." She felt his hug and his tender kiss on her forehead.

"No more than I do, lass, no more than I do." He comforted her. "I will do all I can to protect you, Snow, Cinderella or well, Cyn."

"I know you will." She paused. "Please, Robbie, please also protect the boys."

"Aye, lass, I will," he vowed.

"And tell me, what do you think of Bianca and Walter?" Her curiosity came to the front.

"He is a good man and she must truly love him to get on a horse, so I approve," Robbie decided.

"Me too." This time her smile was real.

Chapter Fifteen

Snow White

They sat on a soft fur Prince Robert had brought with him.
They talked about many things, but for a short while they avoided
two subjects. They did not talk about love because it was too new
and too intense. It also took them some time to begin to talk
about the things happening at the castle. When they did talk
about it, they had much to say.

"Gertrude talks to her mirror!" Snow was agitated. "Some
think it's a magic mirror. In truth, she talks and acts as if it were
answering her but the mirror makes no sound. She is insane,
quite mad."

"What does she say to it?" Prince Robert asked, looking at
her both upset and curious.

"She tells it how she..." As Snow's voice broke with emotion,
she struggled to continue. "How she had my father murdered,
and how she wants me dead too. I hid and listened to her."

"Snow, that was dangerous!" The Prince was shocked.

"I know, but it was necessary." Snow admitted, "And there is
more."

They both paused as the horses whinnied and trumpeted at
each other, pulling against the ties holding them each to a tree.

"What else?" the Prince asked, turning Snow's attention back
to the intrigue.

"My sister Bianca is in love with one of your soldiers,
Walter," Snow told him.

"How do you know this to be true?" he asked her.

"She's been riding out to meet with him daily." Snow smiled.
"Bianca hates riding, hates horses in fact."

There was another pause as the horses strained against the ropes tying them to the tree.

"Snow, would you like to have your mare bred?" Prince Robert asked with some amusement. "If so, let's unsaddle her."

They unsaddled both horses and Snow watched, fascinated, as the Prince led his stallion to the mare. It was both beautiful and frightening to watch, a combination of primitive grace and almost savage desire from both horses. When finished, the horses were silent, and the stallion seemed almost sleepy. Snow felt something stir deep inside her soul.

"Is it always so..." she said tentatively.

"Yes." The Prince smiled at her.

"Robert," Snow said, using his first name for the first time, "would it be that way with us?"

"It would be more passion and more tenderness, and less violent." He looked at her so tenderly her heart beat wildly. "It would be wonderful."

"You mean it will be wonderful," she said firmly, "when it finally happens."

"Yea, it will be." He leaned over and kissed her softly on her lips for the first time. "And I hope it will be soon."

She merely smiled.

They sat once more, each wrapped in their own thoughts until the Prince asked, "What do you think about Bianca loving one of my soldiers?"

"My head guard has spent some time with your soldiers and he tells me the man is a good, decent man," Snow replied. "He is not rich, but he works hard. I am elated for her to have this happiness. I know Gertrude would not approve since the man has no wealth or title."

"Would Bianca wish to wed him?" The Prince looked at Snow with tenderness.

"I believe she would. Bianca on a horse? It must be love, but I would have to ask her," Snow continued, "to be sure and learn her heart."

"I would ask the soldier as well, or have your head guard ask him and report to you," he said slowly, clearly thinking of more than Bianca.

"What are you thinking?" she queried.

"I can arrange for your priest to meet them near the lake on the day after tomorrow and perform the ceremony to marry them," he said with a big smile. Then he hesitated just a moment and continued softly, "Snow, when your priest is marrying Bianca and her soldier, I will have my priest meet us here and marry us, if you would."

Snow felt her heart soar in her chest. "Yes, my Prince, I would."

For the look of sheer joy on her face, she got another kiss, a longer kiss.

Finally, too soon, but finally the Prince pulled away. "Snow, I have another idea, but this one will be hard on you. I will go to the castle for a visit and pretend to be enamored with Gertrude. I will tell her lies to expose the evil in her soul. You must act as though you believe the lies I am telling her."

"Yes, my love, I mean Prince Robert," Snow said quickly. "I have complete faith in you."

"I like it that you called me your love, for you are mine." He smiled into her eyes and continued, "I will pretend to join in her plot to have you murdered, but I will never let that happen. Then your guards will arrest her for the murder of the King and treason."

"But she is the Queen, as least she thinks she is." Snow was confused. "Who can arrest the Queen?"

"I will send a message to my father. I believe he knows the truth about your father's wishes. He had a message from your father shortly before his death."

"My father said he sent a writ with his wishes to someone for safekeeping but he said not who," Snow told him. "It makes sense that he would have sent it to your father."

They parted reluctantly and Snow returned to the castle.

That evening, Snow managed to get Bianca alone. "Tell me about this soldier you have been riding out with. His name is Walter, correct?" At Bianca's nod she continued, "Would you wish to marry him?"

Bianca gave a very dreamy and uncharacteristic sigh. "Yes, but mother..."

"Forget Gertrude," Snow said sharply. "Do you want this man for your husband?"

"Yes, Snow." Bianca's normally strident voice went soft.

"Then the day after tomorrow, you will ride out again," Snow instructed her. "Father Timothy will meet you there and marry you, but you must keep it a secret until then else Gertrude will stop you and probably have Walter beheaded."

"God bless you, Snow." Bianca was laughing with tears in her eyes as she hugged Snow.

Snow watched her as she left the room, feeling the same joy and excitement for herself.

Prince Robert arrived in time for dinner. He secreted himself in a corner with Gertrude, knowing that there were at least two guards and Snow hidden within hearing distance.

"Good evening, Prince Robert." Gertrude gushed so hard that her bosom was about to spill out of her gown. "It seems so long since you last visited."

"Have you really missed me so much?" the Prince asked, flirting.

"It seems an eternity since I have been with you, my Prince." Gertrude rubbed up against him and said, "I love you."

"You flatter me, Your beauteous Highness." Prince Robert fought a rising nausea.

"I would like to marry you, Prince Robert, and join our two kingdoms so we can rule both as King and Queen." Gertrude smiled seductively.

Prince Robert feigned regret. "That would not be possible, Your Highness. I am not the successor to my father's throne. I have an older brother who is next in line."

Gertrude almost cried in desperation, "That is absurd! You would make a much better king than he would!"

This in spite of the fact that she had never seen the Prince's brother, in spite of the fact that the brother did not exist.

"Yes, of course I would," the Prince bragged, "but what can I do?"

Gertrude paced and thought, evil plans were her forte. "I have an idea, we will have your brother marry the brat Snow. There will be a honeymoon voyage..."

"Yes, and then?" the Prince asked.

"And the ship will sink killing all aboard," Gertrude said, excited and loving the idea.

"All?" Prince Robert managed to sound excited, but in truth he felt ill. "You would kill all aboard?"

"We cannot risk any survivors." Gertrude dismissed the thought of killing so many with a wave of her hand. "Yes, then you will be first in line for the throne."

"It's a fine plan," he managed.

"That is not all." Gertrude continued, "Once you and I are married, we can make sure you become king as soon as possible."

"My father is still virile and healthy, he will live for years." The Prince was shocked and horrified.

Gertrude merely smiled and paused without speaking.

"Surely you do not mean that I should kill my own father?" He smiled even though he was sick inside.

"Kill a king? Why not? It would be easy." Gertrude shrugged. "I have done it before."

"We should go into dinner, my love." The Prince was thoroughly repulsed and had to end this conversation.

Dinner that night held a very strange atmosphere. Gertrude was so sure she had outsmarted Snow and won the Prince that she was jubilant, constantly smiling. The Prince was repulsed, planning revenge against Gertrude, but still anticipating his marriage to Snow. His joy won out and his smile was wide and real, which Gertrude in her vanity took for his joy at his plans with her. Snow's anger faded as she thought of marriage to the Prince. Bianca was excited and in love. Bridget was shocked, watching everyone and wondering what was happening.

At one point Bianca took Snow aside. "Snow, dear," she said simply, "can I have Bridget there tomorrow, do you think?"

"I should think so, Bridget is loyal to you, and she loves to ride." Snow continued, "She will keep your secret."

"'Tis good, I will invite her in the morning just before I ride out."

Snow walked out to the barn after dinner. She knew she would not be able to be alone with the Prince without arousing Gertrude's suspicions, however there was a good chance she could talk to her head guard and some of her soldiers. As usual, just by walking to the stables, she found herself met by the head guard and one of his soldiers.

"Milady," the head guard greeted her, "is there anything we can do for you?"

"We know, Milady," the second guard said, smiling. "We know of your plans, and are most pleased for you and for the kingdom. No one is happy with Gertrude as queen."

"I do not accept her as queen, as you both know." Snow was firm.

"As far as the true guards are concerned, to a man they believe you to be the true Queen," the head guard said. "We know Gertrude was behind the murder of your father."

"Has there been talk among the soldiers about taking her prisoner?" she asked.

"Yea, Princess," he replied slowly, "and about killing her, but we want to know who she used to actually do the deed before we take action."

"If I may suggest something," she said softly, "I would look to see any guards who died themselves, shortly after my father's death."

"It will be done, Milady," the guard said with new appreciation for her insight.

"And I have a boon to ask of you." Snow seemed suddenly shy and still filled with joy.

"Anything, Milady." His face was calm, not giving anything away, but he sensed her excitement and it pleased him.

"When I go out the day after next on my daily ride, could you and one of your most trusted guards keep watch, staying behind me and make sure I am not followed?"

"Yes, Milady." He then asked carefully, "Will you be meeting someone on your ride?"

"Yes." She blushed. "I will meet with two people."

"Would it anger Gertrude?" he asked with a small smile.

"Exceedingly so." She met his eyes without guile.

"'Tis good," he said with a wider smile.

"And when Bianca rides out, would you send a couple of soldiers to do the same for her? Make sure no one follows her but Bridget and Father Timothy?"

"Yes, Milady." He paused before asking, "Should Walter be one of the soldiers with Bianca?"

"Yes, he must be." Her smile was wide.

"Will this sting Gertrude as well?" he asked.

"Beyond belief." She grinned at him.

"It will be done, Your Majesty." He bowed before leaving her.

Snow woke that morning both excited and nervous. She hummed as she dressed, choosing a dress that was beautiful and simple. Gertrude would not object to it because to Gertrude every dress had to be covered in lace and jewels to be worth wearing. She was wrong, of course, Snow's beauty did not need lace or jewels.

Snow went downstairs and met with Bianca and Bridget. She

had to work vigorously to persuade her stepsisters not to wear their most elaborate gowns, but she managed to get them to realize that anything more than their normal riding clothes or a simple dress would rouse Gertrude's suspicions. Bridget was confused about what was happening, but since she knew it would prick her mother and make Bianca happy, it was good enough to please her.

"God's blessings on you, Bianca, and you, Bridget." She kissed them both on the cheek.

"And on you as well, Snow." They hugged her and left quickly, neither realizing that she would be married to Prince Robert that very day.

Snow watched as they went to the stables.

She drew a deep breath. Now came the hard part, hiding her delight at the prospect of marrying Prince Robert. For once, Gertrude seemed to want her around, sending her on chores and errands. Snow became both argumentative and inept so that before long Gertrude ordered her out of her sight. Snow ran to the stables.

She gave a quick smile to the stable boy. "I think I will ride the gelding today. I have a secret. I had the mare bred yesterday."

"Bred? To what stallion?" he asked, filled with curiosity.

"I will tell you later." She mounted the gelding and rode off while saying, "It is a most worthy sire."

Although she never looked back, she was well aware of the guards following her. She rode at a steady canter until she got well clear of the castle and pushed the gelding into a hard gallop. She approached the clearing and saw Prince Robert and his priest waiting there. Beside them stood his father and mother, the King and Queen.

The Prince helped her down. "Are you sure, Your Majesty? Once we do this Gertrude will hate you even more. She will try to kill you."

"Again? She already has and failed. Trice, no with the man she tried to force me to marry, four times," Snow told him. "And even one day with you is worth any risk. Yes, I am very sure."

"What has she tried?" He was surprised.

"An arrow barely missed killing me when my father was murdered, I was pushed down the stairs, and when I was in mourning I had no hunger so when I was given a plate of meat I fed it to the dogs." She paused. "I hadn't known that the meat was poisoned, and four of them died."

"Why have you never told me of these attempts on your life?" The Prince seemed almost angry. "It is a life I value very much."

"Because the few times we have been alone," Snow said simply, "I was not thinking of her but of you."

He led her over to his parents. "I am so pleased to meet you, Your Highness, Your Majesty," Snow said with a curtsy.

"We have met before," the King told her as he smiled. "You were just barely old enough to walk. Your father and I always secretly hoped the two of you would marry. I know he would be pleased."

Snow smiled softly but with a few tears forming in her eyes. "Thank you, Your Highness."

"Now tell us all that is happening at the castle." The King was suddenly forceful. "And I will see what I can do to help you end this treachery. I owe your father nothing less."

She sat on a tree stump and began to tell them all.

* * *

Bianca and Bridget reached a clearing by the lake and found the three soldiers and the priest waiting for them. Walter helped Bianca dismount, and to the delight of all kissed her soundly. Bridget was still unaware of what was happening, but she quickly figured it out when the priest began the marriage ceremony that joined Bianca and Walter. She was delighted for Bianca and a bit sad for herself that she had no man to marry.

"Does Snow know?" she asked after kissing and congratulating her sister.

"Snow made the arrangements," Bianca told her, excited and even a bit fearful to make love for the first time with Walter.

"Does Mother know?" Bridget asked as Bianca and Walter moved off.

"No!" Walter answered back just as they disappeared into the brush.

Bridget, the priest and one of the soldiers began the ride back to the castle as the remaining soldier remained at a discreet distance. Walter claimed his bride on a cushion of soft grass using all the tenderness and passion he had inside him. Bianca was ecstatic.

Snow and Prince Robert were married by the river, in the dappled shade from several oak trees. The ceremony was simple, quick, and thrilling. After, they sipped some excellent wine. Then they both signed a parchment and the priest affixed a seal to the bottom. He handed the document back to his king and queen.

"Mother and Father, I am so happy you could be here, and I am thrilled you approve." The Prince kissed his parents. "I am very blessed."

The King and Queen rode off, along with the priest and the soldiers acting as guards. Snow's soldiers left, only to stay a discreet distance away. They kept watch for Snow's safety. They were on the lookout for spies and possible attackers.

Snow looked up at the man who was now her husband and asked shyly, "What do we do now?"

His eager smile startled her. "We consummate the marriage by making love."

"I do not know-" she said very quietly.

"I know you know nothing of what we do now, of making love," he said gently. "If you relax and trust me, I will gladly show you."

So he did. More than once.

"I should have known your father had the writ, my father trusted him," Cyn told Robbie.

"Yes, they were true friends." He put his arm around her shoulder.

Together they watched the horses mating.

"Wow!" Cyn continued, "I never knew animals could have such passion and drama."

"Wait until you see what happens when Snow and the Prince are wed." He laughed.

Her only reply was a soft smile. They listened in as Gertrude plotted to have Prince Robert's non-existent brother killed, along with Snow. The mere thought of it turned Robbie's stomach. Then she told him Gertrude's plan to also kill the Prince's parents.

"She really does not care for anyone save herself." Robbie was astonished. "Her evil has no limits."

"No, Robbie, none at all," she agreed.

"I liked watching the weddings, especially ours," he said with a smile.

"I liked watching the honeymoons, especially ours. Does that make me a peeping Tom?" She laughed, then added on a more serious note, "Will we ever have a honeymoon? Really?"

"I do not know, lass, I pray we do." She felt his kiss, his passion.

Chapter Sixteen

Snow White

It was late when Snow rode back to the castle. She and the Prince knew they needed to keep their marriage a secret until they could fully prove Gertrude was a murderer, have her arrested, and claim her throne from her. Staying apart and hiding the marriage until that time would be hard for both of them.

Snow galloped as she returned to the castle because she knew full well Gertrude would notice how late she was. She tried to think of an explanation but she could not. Fate stepped in and her horse stumbled, falling to his knees and throwing Snow. She walked the rest of the short distance to the stables, noting her horse's slight limp. She and the stable boy knelt and felt the gelding's leg. It seemed to be a minor injury.

"Snow!" Gertrude's strident voice was right behind her. "Where have you been, you worthless hussy?"

"I am sorry, Gertrude, I rode longer than I expected. It was such a fine day. As I was returning my horse stumbled and threw me," Snow said calmly. "We walked back."

Gertrude looked at Snow with her eyes narrowed. "You seem far too happy for having made a long walk home. If I did not know…"

"Know what, Your Majesty?" Snow managed to show respect she did not feel.

"Something is happening," the phony queen said. "I know not what but you are very late and very happy. Even my daughters are acting strange. Bridget seems to be eerily calm, and Bianca… Bianca is very blissful today. She almost glows with it, and she smiles continuously. Something is not right."

"It is not right that your daughters are happy?" Snow asked ingeniously. "I would think a mother would want her daughters to be happy."

"What do you know about anything?" Gertrude replied.

* * *

Snow remembered her parting conversation with the Prince: "Take care, my love. You look far too happy."

"I am very happy, my husband," Snow interrupted with a smile.

"Gertrude will sense your happiness and do whatever she can to ruin it," the Prince said. "If she has the faintest idea of why you are so happy, she may try to kill you yet again. Please, my love, if you sense any danger from her, run! Leave the castle and get away."

"Yes, my love, I will." Snow sealed the promise with a deep kiss.

"If you cannot get to me, find a safe place to hide and keep from her sight," he told her. "I will find you."

* * *

"Never mind," Gertrude said sharply, and brought Snow back to the present. "I will ask my mirror, you lying slut."

It was the first time Gertrude had mentioned talking to the mirror. At a signal from Snow, the stable boy managed to keep his shock to a small gasp.

When Gertrude looked at him the lad said calmly. "My pardon, Queen Gertrude, I found an injury on the gelding's foreleg."

Gertrude left the stables and returned to the castle. Snow followed her into the castle, then went to find her stepsisters. She found them in Bianca's chambers, and Bianca was packing her things to move into a cottage with Walter.

"Does your mother know that you have married?" Snow asked her.

"Not yet, Snow," Bianca said quietly, as if she feared being overheard. "I am so happy but I fear her reaction."

"And rightly so." Snow could not hide a shiver of fear. "You should wait a short time to live with Walter, else you risk both of your lives."

"I know, my sister, but I cannot follow that advice," Bianca replied. "Walter and I plan to leave this place. He has a home with the Prince's father. We will go there."

"Then it went well between you and your new husband?"

"More than well, it was heaven." Bianca paused in her packing and looked closely at Snow. "Snow, you seem extremely happy yourself. Why?"

"I do not know what you mean." Snow tried to dim her smile, without much success. "I am but glad for you of course. Do you want me to distract Gertrude while you leave?"

"That would be best," Bianca said quietly.

"Trust me then, sister." Snow hugged her and left the room, and Bridget followed her.

"Snow, I need to talk to you," Bridget said. "I can see that there is something making you very cheerful. What is it?"

"What do you mean?" Snow wanted to keep her secret.

"If I did not know better I would guess you and Prince Robert..." She gasped. "It is him, is it not? You laid down with him?"

Snow only smiled.

Bridget had a flash of intuition. "You married him even as Bianca married Walter! That is why you were not there!"

"Please keep my secret, even from Bianca," Snow pleaded, "else your mother find out."

"I will." For once Bridget seemed sad.

"What bothers you Bridget?" Snow asked gently.

"You and Bianca have husbands now," she sniffed, "and will soon be gone leaving me alone with Mother. When will I find a husband to love me?"

"You will, I promise." Snow hugged her. "Mayhaps there is someone at Robert's castle who would see the beauty in you."

Snow left to find Gertrude because she needed to keep her distracted. The task proved to be extremely easy. All it took was for Snow to be in the same room with her and keep smiling. After she left Gertrude, she sent a message to the stable boy she trusted.

That night, while Gertrude slept, Snow took the mare and left the castle. She took nothing but a few clothes and her horse. The clothes she took were the childish dresses she had hated so much. She chose them simply because they were more comfortable, and because Gertrude would notice if any of Snow's fine gowns were gone.

Snow knew Gertrude would suspect she had run to Prince Robert, and would send her fastest men after her. Men loyal only to Gertrude. She also knew that if she were caught she would be killed instantly so she went another direction. She was the only one who knew exactly where the boys were and she went to them, taking a roundabout route and making sure she was not followed.

They were in a crude shack with a servant, a teacher, and two trusted guards. Although the shack looked crude, it was extremely sturdy and well supplied. It was also much larger than it looked from the outside. Her father had ordered the hut made so that the natural slope of the land gave part of the hut a second floor. There was also a well-planted garden and some livestock: chickens, two cows, some pigs, and a couple of goats. All were fat and healthy. He had done what he could to see to the boys' welfare.

She rode up and dismounted.

"Brothers!" she called. "It's me, Snow."

They ran out to greet her. It seemed to Snow that they had all grown quite a bit in the few months since she had last seen them. She hugged and kissed every one of them.

"I need a place to hide for a time," she told them. "Can I trust you to keep my secret?"

The boys were all thrilled to have her there and agreed to keep her secret, except from the Prince.

She should have asked the teacher.

Gertrude woke up that morning to find Bianca and all her possessions gone. Then she realized Snow was also gone, but most of her clothes and jewels remained. Bridget cowered and cried when Gertrude questioned her but kept her silence. Gertrude was in a murderous rage.

The stable boy rode off on Snow's gelding, something he often did to exercise the beast. He told the head guard he was going for the Prince.

"Good lad," the guard said. "Do you know where Princess Snow is?"

"Aye, I think so," the lad replied. "I can lead the Prince to her. I believe she is in danger."

Soon after he rode off, a visitor came to see Gertrude. A visitor who expected to be well paid for the information he brought, but instead got his throat cut for his trouble.

When the stable boy arrived at the Prince's castle, he was shown to the Prince instantly.

"What brings you here, lad?" the Prince asked him, his heart racing.

"I came because I fear for Princess Snow," the lad replied. "The pretend Queen, Gertrude, suspects something. I know not what, but she is enraged and Lady Bianca is gone. Now Snow is gone as well. If Gertrude wasn't so angry I would think she had already killed her."

"Do you know where Snow is?" the Prince asked. "Can you take me to her?"

"Aye, I think so," the lad answered. "I think she went to her brothers."

"Snow's brothers?" The Prince was startled.

"The late King had an eye for the ladies," the lad replied. "Snow has seven young brothers of one sort or another."

The Prince immediately ordered two horses saddled, and Snow's gelding cooled down and stabled. He also had some bread, cheese and wine brought out for the boy. He knew something the stable boy had not yet realized. He knew the lad could not go back to the castle as long as Gertrude was there. She would have him killed. He decided to set the lad up in his own stables. He had a quick word with his father who agreed to send his men to finally capture Gertrude. It was past time.

Once the Prince had word his horses were ready, he and the lad went off riding at a gallop.

* * *

Gertrude stood for a moment in front of the mirror, then paused over her collection of potions, selecting one. She easily disguised herself as an old crone simply by removing some of the padding from her bosom. She left her hair down and unpowdered, showing it to be dingy brown with gray streaks. She added a wart to her face, then put on some dirty, tattered clothes, including a gray shawl and a floppy black hat. She nodded to the mirror and left the castle by a secret passageway.

After a few days, Snow took a short walk. She knew better but she felt so agitated and so confined that she was reckless. She was also worried for the teacher, who had gone missing. She feared for his life. She never thought of him as treacherous, but that was a mistake. Fearful and upset, she went out.

She told herself it would be safe to be alone for a short time. She told herself she would stay close to the cottage. She told herself she would be careful. She told herself Gertrude could not know where she was. She was wrong.

Snow rested on a log, thinking about her Prince and wondering how soon they could be together again. She almost drifted off into a warm nap when she was spotted by the crone.

"My lady," the hag said with a high voice that seemed to be hiding a laugh. "You look so beautiful sitting here in the soft sun."

"Thank you, kind woman," Snow replied, but there was a hint of suspicion in her voice. Something about the crone made her uneasy.

"Can I offer you one of these nice apples?" the crone asked.

"Thank you," she told the hag simply, looking into her eyes as she took the apple.

It wasn't recognition of Gertrude's face that did it. It was her eyes, the insanity, and hatred that she could not disguise. Snow threw the apple away.

"Gertrude!" Came her angry sigh.

Gertrude leapt into action, attacking Snow with a small knife. "The apple would have been easier, you stupid child."

She managed to scratch Snow with the dagger she had dipped in poison. Immediately Snow felt weak and dizzy. She fell to the forest floor.

"My husband, Prince Robert, will kill you," she managed.

Even as she gloated in triumph, the words stung Gertrude. She screamed loud enough to flush birds from the trees overhead. Torn between anger and triumph, she made her escape and headed back towards the castle. However her own scream gave her away. The King's men caught up with her long before she reached the castle. The men she had hired to replace the late King's guards were not loyal to the Queen. To a man they surrendered without a fight, and many were more than glad to speak against Gertrude.

Suddenly, 'off with his head' was no longer one of her favorite phrases.

* * *

The boys began to wonder where Snow was. They had no way of knowing how much danger she was in, but they knew something was wrong. They had also noticed, much to their joy, that their teacher was gone. Taking advantage of the unexpected day without lessons, they decided to explore and look for Snow.

They found her, dead, near the log in the woods. They went for their guards. None of them had any idea what had happened to her. The only injury they could find was a small scratch on her arm and a skinned knee, the latter injury from her fall off her horse the day before.

After they cried for a long time, they began the grim task of building her a casket and digging her a grave in the meadow. The two guards helped the boys, carefully and discreetly wiping away their own tears. The maid was crying openly as she helped ready her body for burial.

When it was finally done, the boys stood by the open grave as one of the guards said a quiet prayer. The boys were inconsolable and lost in their grief. Just as the guard was saying, "Amen," they heard hoof beats and looked up.

The Prince came riding into the clearing. Seeing the crude coffin, he jumped down and tore it open. He looked down at Snow, so still, so pale, and felt overwhelmed with grief and an anger beyond belief. He gave her a tender kiss, and then thought he saw her chest rising and falling as she began to breathe again...

"How do you like my brothers?"

"They are scamps, full of life and fun," Robbie replied. "They love you so much."

"For that alone, I believe Gertrude would kill them if she could," she said with some heat in her voice.

"How could Gertrude disguise herself so well?" Robbie wondered.

"It was probably easy. She let her true self show through. She is

ugly in her soul. Any hint of beauty or decency was the real disguise."

She felt Robbie grip her arm. "No, my love, do not eat the apple!"

"She is too smart for that," Cyn said firmly.

They watched as Gertrude scratched Snow with the small dagger. They watched as Snow fell, dead. Cyn felt herself slipping... slipping--

Robbie never felt so alone or so desperate as he did watching the Prince ride up to find Snow dead, her coffin already lowered into the ground.

* * *

He could not stop himself, although it was completely unprofessional. He felt compelled to bend down and give her a soft kiss on the lips.

"Doctor!" The young nurse walked into the room at the worst possible time. She exclaimed, "Did I see you just kiss that patient?"

"I've never done anything like that before." Doctor McDougal was embarrassed. "I couldn't stop myself, I don't even know why I did it."

"It's against all the rules." The nurse was joined by another doctor who spoke up and said, "For good reason."

"Robbie, tell them to stop yelling," came a soft, weak voice. "I'm trying to sleep."

Cynthia Wright Snowden had come out of her coma. Was it the kiss?

Epilogue

So what happened to everyone?

Cyn Snowden married Dr. Robert McDougal in a large but informal ceremony shortly after she was released from the hospital. She had Amy and Jaime as her attendants, along with Robbie's two sisters. Timmy, her youngest brother, was her ring bearer. She still needed more physical therapy and a bit more plastic surgery, but to her Robbie, she was perfect.

When they first met, Robbie's sisters' first question was, "How did you get him to let you call him Robbie? He always hated that."

Cyn just smiled and shrugged her shoulders. "That's what I called him in limbo."

The two women looked at each other then at Cyn with a bemused expression on each of their faces.

Bridget and Bianca both found good, steady husbands, not as spectacular as Robbie, but nice, decent men.

Like her father, Cyn seemed very fertile, she had twins within a year of her discharge from the hospital. This time girls, thank heavens.

It turned out that Robbie had a thoroughbred mare that he decided to have bred to Cyn's stallion.

Gertrude was never arrested, but she did not get away with her crimes. Shortly after Cyn came out of her coma, Gertrude got word she was wanted by the police. She was upset, and being Gertrude, she blamed anyone but herself for her troubles. She had a violent argument with David that turned deadly when he calmly pulled out a knife and stabbed her to death. It was his first act of true violence. He was arrested and convicted of second degree murder.

Cyn and Robbie went to the Kentucky Derby when their first foal was three, and their colt won! Cyn and Robbie, and their children of course, lived happily ever after.

* * *

Cinderella married her Prince and kept him busy and amused because she never lost her humor and spirit. She never really came to be dignified. Prince Robert loved her spirit.

Together they found her late father's fortune, although being married to the Crown Prince made it a moot point. They had no need if it.

Cinderella's mare had a beautiful foal. Bridget married Mr. Alesford, who kept her pregnant for years and in the finest of gowns for the rest of her life. Bianca did not marry for a long time but living in the castle, she finally found a man to love, one who loved her. Gertrude was imprisoned for life, growing old and ugly without her potions. Cinderella and Prince Robert lived happily ever after.

* * *

Snow married her Prince and kept her sense of serenity but added blissfully happy to it. They lived in her castle and his parents lived in theirs, combining the two kingdoms. Snow's mare had a beautiful foal. Snow and her Prince had beautiful children.

Bianca was happily married to her soldier, Walter. Bridget yearned for a husband for years before finding love. The boys moved into the castle with Snow and the Prince and drove everyone in the castle crazy.

The mirror? Snow ordered it destroyed.

Gertrude soon learned that shouting 'off with her head' so many times was a huge mistake.

Snow and her Prince lived happily ever after.

* * *

Once Dauid was dead, Rosie worked to reverse the spell on Robbie. It took her years but eventually she did manage it. He was welcomed back to the village, although most villagers were puzzled. Where had he been? They had thought him dead. Who had died and been buried in Robbie's grave? Rumors and explanations never quite answered the questions, but Robbie's father and his friends were too happy to care. A few years after he woke, he married Rosie's daughter, a lass with long black hair and green eyes, who seemed strangely familiar to him. They lived happily ever after.

Glossary

Breacan-an-feileadh: forerunner to the kilt
Stone put: similar to the modern shot put
Hammer throw: similar to the modern hammer throw
Maide-leisg: a Highland game

Scottish Dialect:
Cannae: cannot
Dinna: do not
Hae: have
Ye/ya: you

Old Scottish names:
Dauid
Thome
Gynne
Mariore

Other books by Susan Kohler

The Heart of The Beast
(historical romance novel)

Working Romance
(contemporary romance novel)

Who's Taming Who?
(contemporary romance novel)

Dreaming of Tomorrow
(contemporary romance novel)

Beautiful in the Lord's Eyes
(contemporary Christian novel)

Note to Readers

Please visit my website at:

http://sueotk2001.tripod.com/susankohlersromancenovels

I have excerpts and information on my novels.

Sue

www.ingramcontent.com/pod-product-compliance
Lightning Source LLC
Chambersburg PA
CBHW020337260626
47156CB00004B/1569